GREGORY EL HARVEY

TO DIE
IN
THE COLDEST
WINTER

I0601914

A NOVEL

Books by Gregory El Harvey

JACKSONVILLE

Autobiographical
FACES IN THE SHADOWS

Serial
THE PATTERN OF A SNOWFLAKE
DRAGONS MORE DECENT THAN MEN
DRAGONS IN LOVE
TO DIE IN THE COLDEST WINTER
THE AUTONOMOUS ASSASSINS

Cover painting: *Three Moons Over the Snow*
by Gregory El Harvey
(www.gregharveygallery.com)

To Jinlong, my very best friend,
who does not care about what I am writing.

ACKNOWLEDGMENTS

I am grateful to Myanna Harvey for critically reading the manuscript and to Cassia Harvey for helping with the publication process.

CHAPTER 1

Philadelphia, Lawncrest, Autumn 2012

Martina Osipov suppressed a pang as the old neighborhood along Rising Sun Avenue came into view. "You know," she remarked, "I should stop telling people my name is Osipov." But after there was no response, she queried, "Are you listening?"

"Yes, dear, I am. *Osipova*, then?"

Wheeling the gray SUV onto a side street, "There are enough Russians here to appreciate the *a*. What do you think?"

"Sure, why not?"

"Talk about noncommittal."

"No, but it's cute, I like it."

"You're thinking of the past, aren't you?"

Margaret Swift-Jones Packard looked out her window at the rowhouses nestled in like living things. Sighing, she answered, "Of course, dear."

Throwing her a glance, "I felt it, too, just pulling onto Rising Sun. Two more turns and I think my heart will stop."

"Let's not be melodramatic, dear, if we can help it."

The turns were made and within moments the SUV, like a quiet lion, moved to the curb. Both women looked toward the familiar front door.

Switching off, Martina pressed her back against the seat. "Twenty years, Maggie."

"Yes, and I thought we'd never leave, except of course, to be taken to hospice. But even then, we'd probably have preferred dying at home."

A sigh. "It's just a house."

"Tell yourself that, dear."

"Memories are powerful, aren't they? But we're just as close now, Maggie, in some ways."

"I suppose."

"You've got Len, and I've got Stanley."

"I love Lenny, as you do your Russian."

"He'd get a kick out of hearing you put it that way."

"Well, I like Stanley, dear." And turning her green eyes to meet the gray eyes, "So, I think I'll let you keep him."

With a chuckle, "Yes, thanks."

A minute later the lion arose, crept down the quiet street, and made its way back into the jungle.

In her NYC office Mary Coldgrave removed her raincoat and hung it up to drip. She did not like the rain, for it produced, at least eventually, mud. Blood she did not mind, but mud, well, what a wretched thing to have in the world. After dropping her purse onto the blotter, she took a seat, swiveled sideways, then opened her phone and scrolled to the O's. But the door opened, so she turned the phone face down and looked up.

"Mary."

"Bob."

"Are your guys going to be all right with this one?"

"Um-hm."

"But they're up-close people, you might consider going at this one from a distance. There can't be mistakes on this one."

She merely offered him a blank expression.

"I know," he continued, leaning against the door frame, "you don't make many mistakes, I understand that, but this one is so important."

She looked at the blue shirt, the tie, the bright, friendly smile, like that of a man who expected everyone to secretly desire to be standing there in his clothes. "I felt," she replied at length, "the targets would probably have to be taken together, that sniping wouldn't work, and that up-close people could do the trick. Up-close work is much more dangerous, I know, especially when dealing with people trained as well as these two are, but it's also more sure. The team should be fine. Besides, every team has to grow."

"Come on, Mary, they're developed, they're mature, what's to grow? This one's really important."

"I know it is. You don't actually have to tell me." She did not bother to hide her annoyance with him, snatching up the phone, as if to dismiss him. How did she ever get into this work? She had never needed to work anyway, but was free simply to attend parties and enjoy life in the sphere around her. As a child she had enjoyed being wealthy, getting new clothes every weekend, eating anything she wanted, swimming in the pool with Bopo, attending seasonal festivies, even going to school, then college, wherever that was, and knowing people and experiencing life. So why exactly had she gone to work in the first place, why had she not resisted more the suggestion of her friends that she experience the real world? But even at that, how in the world had she ended up in the CIA, of all situations. It was all so annoying. She had practically become a policeman.

"Okay, Mary."

"I know it's important," she repeated, "but I'm sure they'll be fine. Besides, I like this team, I like their splash."

He looked at the hair, the eyes, the confident smile, then at the photograph on the wall, of a little girl and a dog beside a swimming pool. Then he simply retreated, pulling the door closed.

When the door closed she lifted the phone and scrolled again to the O's.

"Yes, it is I. ... How have you been, and Stanley, the others? ... Good. ... Yes, I'm fine. But then, what does that mean anyway? Listen, Martina, I have a project for you. I'd like to come tomorrow, yes? ... Good. ... Actually, around three, would that be all right? ... Yes, dinner would be great, thanks. ... Okay, see you all then. ... Surely. Bye."

Then she turned the screen off, shouldered the purse, grabbed the raincoat, and left.

At the front desk she drew her umbrella from the money pot, as the polished copper bucket was called by the other agents, and waited for the secretary's attention. After taking in the sweater, the cleavage, the long dark hair, she told her she was going out for a drink and would return after lunch. But after seeing the woman make a mental note that it was only 9:20, she said she had changed her mind and would not be returning until midafternoon.

The Estate, Lancaster County, Pennsylvania

Martina sipped the dark tea with satisfaction, then looked up and waited for the others to get settled. One by one they took tea and then sat to face the familiar visitor.

Coming in from the kitchen, Maggie asked, "Mary, would you like me to get you some tea?"

"Well, of course, yes, Maggie, that would be superior. But would you have anything to drink with it? Nothing special, of course, perhaps a little gin on ice or something like that."

Martina, familiar as she was with Coldgrave's aristocratic manner, still could not resist reacting to her tone with a raise of her eyebrows. Surreptitiously she took in the expensive clothes and shoes, the beautiful face, the sumptuous lips impeccably lipsticked in deep red. It was the eyes, of course, that had stolen everyone's attention at the first meeting nearly a year earlier. While the right eye looked at you the left ran out to the side, which oddly added to the woman's natural beauty a certain sensuousness that bordered on sensuality.

"Surely," replied Maggie, "and I have the party ice, just for you. Sapphire?"

"Perfect," answered Coldgrave, crossing her legs and running her right eye over the members of the team.

Martina cleared her throat. "So, Mary, what's the deal?"

She did not answer immediately, but chose rather to let her gaze rest for a moment upon the soft luster of the platinum hair. Martina Jung Osipov. At seventy-three, considered by many in the Agency to be a little overdue for retirement. But obviously still attractive and demonstrably viable as team leader. Besides, adored by her husband Stanley. Stanley Osipov. A curious man, sensitive, intelligent, ten years younger than Martina. Formerly a photographer for, but not with, the KGB. Surely, half a communist. Then, Gretchin Wheeler. Fifty-seven, savvy, sexy, verbally abusive. Volatile to the point of appearing untrustworthy. Then, Bradley Hopkins. Forty-five years old going on eighteen. Ex-Air Force, cocky, patriotic, proud of his father, who had died in Vietnam. Chases Gretchin. Then, Bobbie Lee Henry. Thirty-four years old, muscles, piece of work. Ex-specialist for the Memphis police. Prowess with weapons and motorcycles. Then, Kelly Connors. Acquired out of Ireland through a special deal. Cold inside, killer of the first order, blond, beautiful, thirty-nine years old. Invaluable. Then, Martina's long-time friend Margaret Swift-Jones Packard. Retired from field service with the team, now housekeeper. Sixty-eight, intelligent, objective, precise, very old-school. Finally, her husband, the notorious Leonard Packard. Sixty-four, crotchety, even mean. Professional, occasionally pressed into field service, but semi-retired and now in charge of the team's weapons maintenance, ammunition supplies and onsite gun range.

"Mary," Martina repeated, as if to bring the other back to herself, "the project?"

Taking the glass from Maggie, Coldgrave replied, "Yes, the project, of course. I think you will all enjoy yourselves on this one. A challenging job can be more fun than an easy one. Anyway, your targets will be two women, both ex-military, who know their weapons exceedingly well. They are very dangerous." Here she paused, put the glass to her nose, and with closed eyes breathed in the alcohol.

Clearing her throat, Gretchin, said, "So, what did they do?"

"Ah," returned Coldgrave, grimacing, "one doesn't have to *do* anything to get on the Agency's list, not really. Actions alone don't necessarily define a menace."

Giving the dragon tattoo on her neck a delicate scratch, as if to consider this statement, Gretchin said, "*Menace* as in the dictionary?"

"Yes, the one published by the Agency, of course."

"Why use the word, then? It sounds moralistic."

A little shrug, pretty, nearly coquettish. "Just for color."

Gretchin sniffed. "Yeah, sure, but you want us to kill these people, right?"

"I'll get to that, Gretchin, just be patient, listen to the background, if you would."

"Kill," insisted the other. "Let's face it, we are a murder squad."

With a look of distress, Coldgrave set the glass down. "Well, I think a better way to describe the team would be to say you are agents of the state, angels of mercy, so to speak."

Hooting, Gretchin pushed a handful of red hair behind an ear. "Oh my God, *mercy, angels,* really? Jesus, that's a stretch."

"Please, Gretchin," put in Martina impatiently, "just listen, okay? Mary, continue."

But Coldgrave, showing no interest in being hurried, took a long moment to finish the gin, then tipped the glass up farther to glean the last few drops. Maggie was at her side before the ice settled. Taking the glass to the kitchen, while everyone waited, she soon returned with a fresh drink. Nearly immensely pleased, Coldgrave took the glass and looked down into it, as if peering into a magic well.

"You know," she remarked with consideration, "if you really like the term *murder squad,* that's fine with me. I'm not sure the Agency will go for it, but I'm good with it. . . . But as I said, before, this couple is very dangerous and to be approached only with professional caution. The one seems to be a bit of a genius, while the other somewhat of a brute. They've been on our radar for some time, and I'm afraid their number has come up. Anyway, they are into selling explosives, so, enough said right there. They have killed at least three people in their dealings. In any case, they are your targets. They must not be caught, arrested, you understand, which would be very bad. When people like this go to prison, they make contacts that can exponentially increase the menace."

"We understand, Mary," said Martina, "we know the protocol very well."

"I'm sure you do, but here it needs to be stressed. They are *not* to be captured."

"Got it."

"And no standoff, which might be tricky. Intel says they're very well armed."

Maggie, seated beside her husband, the grizzled Packard, leaned forward. "Could you be more specific, Mary? How well armed?"

"Oh, probably a number of .223's, full auto, of course, who knows how many handguns, both suppressed and not, frag and incendiary grenades, and maybe even some C4, who knows?"

"So, you're talking war."

Coldgrave took another taste of the gin. "That would be an accurate term, yes. Their military backgrounds indicate they were somewhat comparable to SEALs, but not as nice as SEALs, if you get the picture."

"In other words," Packard growled, exposing yellowed teeth, "they don't need a gun to kill you, but with a gun they can kill all of you. I've met the brand."

She gave the wolfish teeth a second look. Perusing the field reports in his file had been a colorful experience and had told her explicitly what this gruesome man could do, how for instance he had gone into a room with five armed mob guys and with a single seven-shot magnum had killed them all. Using a tool like this cold-blooded man was like having the devil preach the gospel—everybody in the room would convert on the spot.

But he had caught her look and now returned it icily, for he had met her brand before, too, and knew that at core she was as cold as he was, perhaps colder. Then, uncrossing his arms, as if to unveil the two jackass-rigged magnums strapped over the short-sleeved white shirt, he turned to the Russian and grunted, "You'll need your Tokarev."

Osipov grinned and replied, his accent unusually heavy, "I will take it."

But Maggie, with a shake of her head, said, "We could easily lose somebody."

A slight shrug from Coldgrave, then, "You people are pretty lucky, and creative, you've proven that."

Bradley, who had been pulling lint from his pants, said, "Yeah, we'll be all right, it's just the two of them, right?"

Gravely, Martina queried, "Who do you want on this one, Mary?"

"Everybody except Len and Maggie," was the reply. "I know you enjoy working on the projects, Mr. Packard, but officially you're both retired. This is a pretty important fort to hold down, and the funds aren't there for another housekeeper or guard. There's too great an arsenal here, so except for an emergency—"

With a rudish sniff, Packard folded his arms again. "Sure, I don't give a dog's drool. I'll plant some flowers or something."

Maggie frowned. "It's autumn, Lenny, you're thinking of spring."

He shrugged. "Whatever."

Gretchin straightened herself. "Speaking of a housekeeper, I think we need someone else to help with things."

"But I only mentioned it," replied Coldgrave, "to emphasize the lack of funding."

"This house is too big for Maggie to keep up with. It's not reasonable to ask her to do it all. Now, I clean my own room, but that's miniscule. There are two houses here and many stairs, and with two dogs, well, it's too much for one person."

"What would be required?"

"Someone to come in once a week, say. Maggie, would that be helpful?"

Maggie, turning a little pink, replied, "Yes, that would be very helpful. The vacuums are heavy."

"So," said Gretchin, looking at Coldgrave, "could you put in a request?"

"All right, Gretchin, Maggie, I will submit the request as soon as I get back to my office."

Martina then asked, "Mary, where are the targets?"

"Oh yes, well, actually they are in Florida, a place called Sanibel Island. They have a house there in a quiet neighborhood close to one of the shell beaches. People go to the island to collect seashells. I've never done that myself, look for seashells, I mean, but I'm sure people enjoy that kind of thing."

"Are we looking for information, computers?"

"Of course not. Now you should all know, there are quirks about the island that you will have to accommodate. It's a semi-natural habitat for turtles, of all things. Look it up, find out what you can, but you might have considerable nonsense to work around. I'll send photos of the targets and more info later, but basically they spend their leisure time collecting shells from the beaches and doing snorkeling in the Gulf. Occasionally they make motorcycle trips inland, presumably on business. . . . It would be good, I think, if you all went down as vacationers. Take the SUV, you know, with bikes on a rack, the way people do, with the four of you in one vehicle. Bradley and Gretchin should take the yellow car and go as vacationers, too, a married couple. I'll arrange a place for you to stay, so don't worry about that. It all must be cleared by security, you understand."

"Yellow car?" repeated Bradley, wincing. "It's a Corvette."

Somewhat contemptuously, she replied, "Yes, of course, a Chevrolet. . . . But you must all be careful. These people are Ops. They're smart and suspicious, and if you lose them, we'll never find them. Escaping into the Gulf at night or into the Everglades would not be a challenge for them, it would be just another exercise. You cannot lose them, you cannot. I would suggest taking only the necessary risks and avoiding any bravado. Martina, please call me with your plan a few days after receiving the info packet. Good luck, everybody, you'll need it."

Following dinner, Coldgrave threw a tweed cloak around her shoulders and bade them good-bye, at which theater Martina and Maggie recoiled in unison. As she got into the Jaguar she said, "I only hope it turns over and gets me home. I'm sure it will."

"She seems to like saying that," observed Martina as the engine came to life. "Someone should let her know how effected that sounds."

Maggie smiled. "I'm afraid she's in another world, dear. People like that cannot be reached." Watching the taillights disappear, she said, "Do you think we should have let her go, with that much alcohol in her? She drank all through dinner too."

"Anybody else, no, but her, well, I'd say she'll be fine."

"What I want to know is how she can drink like that and stay slim."

"And sexy. God, I think the men could smell her across the room, and I don't mean her perfume. I'm surprised they didn't follow her to the car."

Maggie smoothed back her Presley-cut hair. "You know, there is something odd about Mary, something I can't quite define, and yet something distinctly attractive."

"Attractive to you?"

"Yes, in a way. I don't know what it is, but yes, attractive."

CHAPTER 2

Sanibel Island, Florida, June 2013

The sun beat blisteringly upon the bug-spattered Corvette as it crossed the causeway toward the island, turning the car's normally pretty yellow into an ugly sulfuric gleam. In fact, the burning color was so intense as to compel Gretchin to put her sunglasses on as she looked out over its hood. And from the water glinted terrible sparkles of colors that even the artist in her could not identify.

"God, this is real," she remarked as they reached midpoint on the causeway. "Every thing I see hurts. That's intense, right, Brad?"

With a frown, "You never call me that, except to make fun of me. You incessantly call me Bradley to torment me. So, I know something's wrong. What is it, what did I do, what did I say?"

"You sound gun-shy."

"Yeah, a little, around you. Who wouldn't be?"

Ignoring this, she said, "*Incessantly*? You actually use four-syllable words? I'm impressed. Next you'll be looking them up to know what they mean."

"I went to college, I was in the Air Force, *not easy*, I can say that. And I was the principal in the school you taught at for how many years? *I* was *your* boss in an academic place. Why do you make me out to be dumb and ignorant?"

"*Academic*? It was a middle school, Bradley."

"Yeah, well, so?"

"You tell people you were a principal at an academic institution? Most of the kids in my class just made paper airplanes."

Ignoring her, "Listen, I know and use big words, okay?"

"Oh, that's not a big word, Bradley, just a four-syllable one. Put it away and zip up, okay?"

With a shake of his head, "Boy, you can be mean. . . . Can you see them?"

"You've got a mirror, too," she said, pulling her visor down and angling its mirror to take a look. "No, I can't, but the text said they've seen us."

As the car finished the causeway and entered the island a bird somewhere lifted its head and peered over the edge of its nest, a dog in some yard arose from a mat and slank over to a waterbowl, and an aligator, one of the myriad which deemed the island their territory, crawled from under a palmetto and slipped into a cooler, marsh habitat.

The Sanibel Palm Cottages were accomodating but not immaculate. There were no amenities to speak of, unless free coffee at the office counted as such. But the crucifying heat and humidity usually precluded the attraction of hot coffee. The little cottages contained each a bed, a desk, a lamp, an old TV, a tiny shower, and a minimally effective window air conditioner. There was a small swimming pool behind the cottages, which showed its age by its cracked and algae-stained concrete.

Tossing her suitcase onto the bed, Gretchin wrinkled her nose. "Tell me I can't smell mildew."

"You've got a nose, I can say that."

She stopped unzipping the case. "What's that supposed to mean, Bradley boy?"

"Not a big one," he replied, "a sensitive one, one that smells out things."

"Right, sure. Look, smartass, we're supposed to be husband and wife, so yes, we can squabble, but watch your goddamn step, okay? It's going to be a long ride home and I can write your name on the board any time I want, so watch it, prick."

"Don't talk dirty. But speaking of, um, you know what, when are you going to say yes to me?"

"Marriage?" she returned, unzipping the case the rest of the way. "And I should be so lucky?"

"Ah, come on, think about it, it could be wonderful."

She gave him a look. "Yeah, like waking up with you every morning, your crank in my hand, sure."

"So, you're saying no?"

"I have to go to the bathroom, could you just take a walk or something, maybe a long walk? And turn that thing on, it's hot as hell in here. It probably doesn't work. This place is kind of shabby, I think. What is it with the Agency anyway, look at this dump. God, I'm sweating like anything. We should have done this thing last fall. Why is it so damned hot down here? The humidity must be crazy, probably ninety."

"Yeah, seems pretty hot. But there's a pool and you'll get to swim, wear a bikini, maybe even part of a bikini."

She gave him another look. "Don't, just don't. And hey, bub, a little privacy, please, like now, okay?"

He switched the air conditioner on and left. The Corvette's bug-strewn windshield, which seemed nearly opaque, and its besmirched paint caused him pain as he stepped to the gravel and headed for the office.

"Hello again," offered the attendant, a loud, confident Ukrainian man. "Is everything okay?"

"Yeah, yeah, perfect, just came for coffee."

"Help yourself, nobody wants it, just spring water from cooler."

With a cup in hand, he said, "I read there are aligators here."

"That is correct, and they can be dangerous. Do not feed them or get too close. There are signs."

"And what's the turtle thing?"

A big grin. "They are everywhere. Be careful, they are more dangerous than the aligators."

He took a sip of the coffee. "How so?"

"If you hurt one of them, even by mistake, the nature people will practically string you up. And no lights at night, no flashlights or anything like that, especially on the beach, because when the eggs hatch the babies will go to light instead of to ocean. It is very big deal here."

"Gotcha." After draining the cup, he walked to the window and looked out to see the gray SUV enter the driveway. He smiled to himself, for the bicycles racked upon the car's rear gate gave the party a distinct vacationers look. "Is the pool open?"

"Sure. Take woman for swim, she will love it, and then to restaurant. There are so many restaurants here, you will not believe it, great choices. It will be very nice, trust me."

At Stanley's touch Martina lowered her menu and looked up to see Connors and Bobbie Lee come in, who had decided to ride their bikes the short distance to the restaurant.

With a roll of her eyes, Bobbie Lee said, "Not doin' this again, no way, bicycles are too slow, I can tell you that right now. Every block feels like a mile."

Connors, her Irish accent heavy, added, "Et's batter'n ridin' a motorcycle all the way to Florida. That would've been nuts, me butt would've hurt for a year."

"Don't complain about ridin', girl, drivin's the real work. Besides, I take all the bugs and road shit."

Looking over his menu, Stanley offered, "I once rode a horse for four hours with a woman on the back. I could not walk for one more hour."

"You never told me that," said Martina.

He smiled. "I did not want to bore you."

"And where was this?"

"Near to Moscow. I was young, it does not matter, but I am thinking it was like riding a motorcycle from Pennsylvania."

"With a woman on the back."

"Correct."

"And you would enjoy doing that, I'll bet."

"I suppose you are correct again," he replied, "if you would be the woman."

She loved him when he was like this, light-hearted, happy, making frivolous jokes. How often she had wanted to thank someone, anyone, even God or nature, for this man who could appreciate, navigate and engage with both the drama and the comedy of life. Looking at him now, with his wire-rimmed glasses and short-cropped beard, she easily recalled those first days when they fell in love. Bobbie Lee's voice brought her back to herself.

"Listen, four hours on horseback wouldn't be nearly as hard as ridin' a motorcycle from Pennsylvania to here, even with a girlfriend on the back."

"She was not my girlfriend."

Martina laid a hand on his arm. "Well, I'm happy about that."

When Gretchin and Bradley arrived Martina passed them a menu and took an obvious read of her watch. Gretchin, scooting her chair closer to the table, only said, "We were arguing."

It was two days later that a bottle of wine was opened in Connors' and Bobbie Lee's cottage, with the general hope of quelling the team's frustration with the project. From whichever vantage point they had explored, the same conclusion had been reached, that intel had been correct in one vital aspect of the targets' habits, in that the two rarely emerged from the house together or went anywhere together. Whether collecting seashells along the island's beaches, shopping, or simply gassing up the car, they seemed to do everything separately.

"It is obvious," said Stanley, pouring wine into their glasses as they held them forth, "if we cannot get them together, one will be escaping. This is probably why they do it. They are sneaky, like Russians."

Bradley, holding out his glass, said, "So, what about the motorcycle trips?"

The other shook his head. "We cannot wait for that, we will be here too long. If we are here too long, people will see we are not taking the vacation, they will become suspicious."

"I agree," said Martina, "we cannot afford to wait. And we should not expect to get lucky with these people."

Bradley lifted his glass. "As in the Manayunk project? Why not?"

"Because," Stanley answered, "it would be playing with the logic."

A grin. "You mean, the odds."

"No, the logic. It is not logical to expect to roll the snake eyes twice."

"Okay, *boys*," put in Gretchin, "so what do we do? Kelly?"

Bradley stiffened. "Why not ask me, Gretchin, what's wrong with asking me? I'm your partner, am I not? You never ask me anything, do you know that, have you ever realized that? You never ask me my advice, my opinion, or anything. I have ideas, too, you know." Then he turned away, slurping his wine.

"God, what a child," she returned, "what a pathetic child of a man. You drive a Corvette, shoot a .45, and talk nothing but bullshit all day long. Everything you say, yeah, and everything you've ever said, is stupid. You act like a teenager on steroids, and you expect me to ask you for ideas? Get real, Superman."

"Well," observed Connors with unusual levity, "at least yous two won't have your cover blown, yous act loike a married coople all the time."

"Oh, shut up," he blurted back at her, "who asked you, miss Sinn Fein?"

She tilted a thumb toward Gretchin. "She joost ded, fucker, or was that too long ago for you to remamber?"

His face red, he turned away from her, muttering, "Little Irish schoolgirl, go back to your convent."

Deftly she stepped up behind him and slapped him hard across the back of the head.

"Ow!" he yelled, whirling round. "Dammit, that hurt. What'd you do that for?"

Her pale skin glowing as she fixed him with her colorless eyes, she said, "You got on me bad side, you fuckin' piece of shet."

"That's a threat," he blustered, "that's a threat, you all heard it, she threatened me."

There was a hush as she said fiercely, "I told you once, fucker, I don't t'reaten people, I kell tham."

He did not respond, but simply looked into the glimmering eyes.

Stepping forward, as if to come between them, Martina said, "All right, listen, let's get ourselves together here. Kelly, what do you think, and I'm asking her, Bradley, not you, so, live with it. Kelly, Bobbie Lee, any ideas?"

The latter flexed the muscles in her forearms, causing them to ripple as she stared at Bradley. Then she said, "Gritchin, you'd better stand guard on this moron, or I might jist beat him to death sometime, and I won't hide the body, I'll drag it out in the street so people can urinate on it."

Bradley grinned. "Oh, now I have her threatening me, too. Who's next?"

Martina put her glass down. "Shut up, Bradley, just shut up. Kelly, how about it?"

Connors held her glass out for the Russian to replenish. "I'm not sher. We can't go tryin' to gat ento the house, et's prob'ly death trapped, and ef not, they'd kell us for sher thamsalves."

"How about a trick, like your utilities thing, with the clipboard?"

"Coldgrave said they're suspicious, and I believe et. They're Ops people, and Ops are hard to fool. We could attampt to steal their car, and they might come out togather."

Martina looked at her, then at Stanley.

Later that night, the Russian rolled over in bed, put his arm over her and kissed her neck. "Russians always kiss neck of the wife, then they kiss something else."

"Um-m, that is what I need," she whispered.

"And why are you needing it?"

"Because I am feeling old. I should retire. I think I'm going to retire after this project." As he did not respond, she continued, "Seventy-three is when people die, let alone retire."

Softly he kissed her neck again. "You are feeling weak?"

"Yes. Especially after this evening. Weak and slow thinking."

"You are a good team leader. You speak with authority, that is enough. It was you, not the younger ones, who stopped the fighting. You were needed tonight, much needed. Please do not retire. Besides, I love you."

"What does that have to do with it?"

"I am not certain," he said softly, "but I will think of something. Give me time, I am not as young as I used to be."

"You're ten years younger than I am. You're not making sense, crazy Russian."

"Actually," he continued, "if you want to do the retirement, we could move to Italy, where we were very happy. You liked it there."

"I did."

Then he moved his hand over her body as he whispered, "Good night."

"No you don't, not yet."

Through the darkness Bobbie Lee whispered, "You asleep, Killy?"

A sigh. "No."

"You thinkin' 'bout, killin' Bradley?"

"No, I was joost t'inkin' of me ma."

"Well, that boy had better shut his mouth, or I'm liable to make Gritchin a widow before she's married. I hate that guy. . . . Are you okay?"

"Yeah. Joost t'inkin' 'bout me ma."

"You've got yourself a soft heart, girl, you know that?"

"No."

"Anything else you're thinkin' about?"

"No."

"Know what I've been thinkin'? We could come back down here sometime and collect seashills. Ever do that?"

"No."

"Want to?"

"Sher."

"I've never seen so many seashills as they've got here. You saw 'em, the whole beach is covered with 'em." And after a moment, "Good night, Killy."

"Good noight."

Switching off the bathroom light, Gretchin looked through the darkness at the bed. She could see him lying there in the faint light that filtered through the window. She sat on the edge of the bed and pushed her slippers off. After waiting to feel the air conditioner's breeze, she lay back and pulled the sheet over her.

"You asleep?" she whispered.

"Nope."

"The wine was good tonight, even with the fight, wasn't it?"

"I guess."

"Good night, Bradley."

"Yep."

CHAPTER 3

The sun broke clear and strong as it climbed over the trees and began to shine upon the beach and the myriad of new shells washed ashore during the night. As the sharp edges of broken shells cut into her shoes, Martina forced herself to concentrate on her search. For all its beauty, its glorious breast decorated with baubles, the Sanibel beach could be a treacherous place. She stooped to pick up a complete angel wing and beside it a mossy ark. Carefully she placed them on top of the other shells in her plastic bag.

She was not alone on the beach, and many of the collectors and combers scouring within earshot had been there since dawn. Upon a greeting from behind her, she turned and presented a quick smile to a sixtyish woman in a straw hat, oversized T-shirt, shorts, and flipflops. She carried no bag but a long walking stick. A small shovel dangled from her belt.

"I see," she said in a husky voice, "that you're collecting."

"Yes, and you?"

The woman took a moment to lean upon her stick, as if about to launch into a story. "No, I've got a house full of them, I don't need any more, thank you. I'm here for the turtles, that's what I do. If you see them crawling down to the water, don't get in their way. We care for our turtles around here. And be careful not to step on one either."

"I'll be careful."

"Do that. And have a good day. We're the seashell capital of the world right here, so enjoy yourself." With that, she lifted the stick and began to walk away, as if on a pilgrimage, but soon stopped and turned back to say, "You can spray your shells lightly, dry them in the sun, and hot glue them onto a board. They'll look real nice."

"I will, yes, thanks."

The woman continued her walk for a good distance, occasionally stopping to talk to people, then stopped, pulled a phone from her shorts and placed a call. Martina closed and tied the top of her bag, then opened her phone and texted Stanley that she had an odd feeling and was heading back. Then she began to make her way over the shell-littered sand, back to the bike she had left at street's end. Pushing a palmetto aside, she stopped among the trees and bushes to read his return text that he was bringing the car.

Closing the phone, she looked up.

He found her there, her body fallen, the phone still in her grip. He could not see her face, for it was covered by palmetto branches, and something stopped him from moving them aside. Then he saw her hand move and he fell to her side, frantically moving the branches from her face as she looked up at him. A mass of blood covered her abdomen and dripped from her mouth. She was choking as she looked at him through glazed eyes.

"Oh God, oh God, no, no, no!" he muttered. "Oh God, no, please no, please no." And he began to weep, pressing his face into her blood-soaked shirt.

"Stanley," she said feebly, "it was a woman, about sixty, a walking stick, flipflops. She called them after talking to me, I think, then I left and one of the targets just appeared, right over there. She shot me, three times, I think, and kept walking. . . . God almighty, God almighty, I hate it here. . . . Look at me, my hair, oh, oh my God, Stanley. I love you, Stanley. I hate it here, it's so hot." But he only wept uncontrollably, and she said, "Oh, Stanley, why could I not die in the snow, in the winter, the coldest winter?"

He put his hands under her, but she went limp. For a moment he continued to hold her and look at her through his tears, the blood dripping from her mouth. Then he let her go and covered his face with his bloodied hands and wept.

Within minutes Bradley and Gretchin were there. The three laid Martina's body in the back of the SUV, placed the bike back on the rack, and drove back to the cottages.

They left her under a blanket, with the air conditioner on high, and went inside to call

Coldgrave. Connors and Bobbie Lee had weapons spread upon the bed, where Martina had slept, and were checking ammunition. When Stanley came out of the shower, his face swollen from crying, he said he needed something to drink. Gretchin offered him a bottle of water, but he refused it, saying he needed something to drink. Connors left and brought him back a beer from her fridge.

Within an hour after the call to Coldgrave a sedan pulled in beside the SUV. Two men in khakis and sport shirts placed Martina in a body bag and took her away. As Stanley watched from the window, for the others had not wanted him to go out again, he thought of being back in Russia in winter. He continued to watch as the Ukrainian man talked with the others outside, then went back to his office.

Bobbie Lee brought in more beer, and the discussion was begun, a discussion everyone had always known was possible but still never expected to happen. Placing her bottle on the bedside table, Connors spoke.

"Coldgrave was blunt about et," she said, "Osipov is now team leader. As a killer I wasn't suited, she said, to be team leader. So, there you have et, Russian, steer the shep."

For a moment, he sat silent, the bottle in his hand, then he said, "And what should I be doing with this? Martina was perfect, so caring for the team, so wise for the projects. What should I be doing with this, please tell me?"

The others simply looked at him helplessly, but Connors said, "Well, you moight try a lettle fuckin' revange." And tipping the bottle, she calmly took another drink and watched him.

Nearly a minute passed. Breaking the hush, the Russian said, "I do not think we are suspected."

Momentarily, Gretchin asked, "How do you know? This was brutal, Stanley, we'd better be very careful here. We'd been to restaurants and other places with Martina, we must have been seen."

He shook his head. "They would never have gone for her like that, I think. They would not have isolated her and only sent one person, they would have come more after the group, all of us. They would not have done the very thing we did not want to do with them and get us one by one. It would have been bad strategy. I do not think they even suspected her, they were just willing to kill her to make sure."

Rubbing his chin, Bradley said, "I don't know, Osipov. I'm so sorry about Martina and everything, but I have to say, that sounds a little off to me."

"And," said Stanley, putting his forefinger up, "the woman on the beach, who made the call, she would not have been wearing the flipflop shoes, she would have been wearing sneakers, something stronger, I think."

Bradley shook his head in doubtfulness. "Ah, no, Stanley, that sounds off to me, I don't know. Too much is at stake here, we have to be careful. They could be coming for us right now."

"No," said the Russian, "I do not think so. They will be wary, that is certain, but I think they just took the chance and killed her, that is all."

Gretchin, who had been staring at Stanley, said, "Okay. So, what do you think about that, Kelly, Bobbie Lee, does what Stanley says sound right?"

Connors screwed the top from another bottle, let the beer chug, then wiped her mouth with the back of her hand. "Sounds roight to me, sounds roight on the mooney."

"Yip," chimed Bobbie Lee, "it sounds right to me too."

"Besoides," added Connors, "I don't gev a fuck ef et's not roight, I'm goin' for t'ese people, and aven ef I have to sattle for one of 'am, I'm kellin' her on the spot and burnin' the house to the ground."

Bradley swallowed at this.

Bobbie Lee said, "The file said they're both Northerners. Well, I'm from Tinnessee and I hate Yankees."

"But," said Bradley, "we're from the North."

But she only looked at him.

"All roight," said Connors, looking at Stanley, "how 'bout et, Russian, what's the plan?"

"I am not certain," he replied, looking back at her, "I am thinking that you might all get hurt."

She took another swig from the bottle. "I t'ink they're both en that house roight now. After kellin' Martina, I t'ink they're both joost goin' to stay there for a day or so and not go anywhere. So, I'll naed Bradley to cover the back, Osipov the garage soide, and Gratchin the other soide. I'm blowin' me way en the front door, and Bobbie Lee's comin' en behind me. I may be kessin' the Holy Vairgin shartly, but I'm sendin' at least one of tham fuckers to hell fairst."

"That's all right, girl," chimed Bobbie Lee. "You sind one, I'll sind the other."

Gretchin herself now swallowed. "When do you want to do this?"

Connors looked at her and replied, "As soon as I'm fenished me fuckin' beer." But then she said to Stanley, "You're the team leader, what d'you say?"

The Russian, his head down, answered, "We should do it now." And looking around at them, he said, "Get everything into the cars quickly. Leave the bikes."

Easing the Corvette around the corner, Bradley pulled to the curb and moved the shift to neutral. When the SUV rounded the corner at the opposite end of the block and stopped, he pulled the shift into drive, his eyes searching for neighbors and other cars. "Okay," he said, "wait for the call."

Gretchin sniffed. "I know that, Bradley, don't tell me what to do. And turn the air up."

He looked over at her. "Are you crying?"

Again she sniffed. "Maybe just a little, asshole." Then her phone rang and she answered it. "That's at the third house in? Yeah, I see him, he's watering his lawn, I think. . . . Wait a minute, here's a kid on a bike, hold on." Getting out, she called, "Hey, kid, where do you live?"

"Windview Avenue," he answered, getting off the bike.

Then she said to him forcefully, the open phone still in her hand, "Go home right now, go, get out of here! Get out of here, I'm coming after you! Get going now!" As he frantically dragged the bike sideways, then got on and began to ride, she got back into the car. As he rounded the corner and disappeared she said, "He's gone, Stanley. . . . Right, okay." Then she closed the phone and said to Bradley, "He said go now."

Both cars were pulled to the curb one house away from the targets' house and the engines left running. Immediately the doors were opened.

Gretchin, Bradley, and the Russian moved quickly toward their positions, where they drew handguns, but Connors and Bobbie Lee, each with a semiauto shotgun, were now at the front door. Simultaneously they fired at the door's plate glass until it was blown away, then cleared the fragments with the butts and stepped inside the house. Looking askance, Gretchin watched the man with the hose for activity, but he only watched her back, turning the hose upon the bushes.

For half a minute no sound came from the house. But then a terrific rattle of gunfire and yelling erupted, lasting for about twenty seconds. Gretchin, her 9 mm aloft, covering the windows, called to Bradley, "Anything yet?"

"No," he called back, "but shoot anybody coming out a window."

"I know that, Bradley!" she yelled, her heart pounding.

Suddenly Connors stepped out through the blown-in front door. "Ever'body stay there," she ordered. "Osipov, come haire!"

Lowering the Glock, Gretchin took a few steps back, until she could see Bradley. His 1911 was still up.

"Don't look at me," he said, "watch the windows."

"I know that, Bradley," she returned, bringing the gun back up. Then she saw a woman walking toward her from the sidewalk, a phone in her hand.

"What's this, police work?" queried the woman amiably, "or are you doing a video or something? There's apps for capturing things like this. I'm from the house over there." But when Gretchin moved the gun slightly in the woman's direction and commanded her to leave, she turned sharply, although still unperturbed, and made her way back to the sidewalk.

Seconds later, the Russian stepped backward through the door, Bobbie Lee clinging to his neck, hobbling on one foot. Connors, carrying the shotguns, followed them and called, "Lat's go, ever'body out."

Even before the cars were moving, the house began to burn, and as they crept away, as if quietly heading for church, black smoke began to pour from the side windows. Through the Corvette's rear glass Gretchin could see the woman, still on the sidewalk, her phone held high as she videoed the burning house.

They did not return to the cottages, but drove toward the causeway. Connors took Martina's place as navigator beside Stanley. The sun was still high as the two cars finished the causeway. The Corvette then headed inland to begin the homeward trip, while the SUV, as directed by Coldgrave, headed for HealthPark Medical Center.

Four hours later, with Stanley taking the wheel for the first leg of the trek, they headed further inland to return home. "What is behind us?" he muttered. "I do not know yet what is behind us. I will not know until my dreams of her come to torment me. My God, what has happened to her?"

Connors looked at him, wondering how many times Martina had seen his profile like this. "You doin' okay?" she asked softly. He did not respond, and she did not ask further, but pulled her visor down and looked at herself in the mirror. Turning it, she caught Bobbie Lee's eyes from the back seat and behind her the shiny edge of aluminum crutches. "Kaep a watch on that bandage for blood," she said. "That lag's gonna hurt for some toime."

"Yeah, .223's can be real mean. At three thousand feet per second, nothin' much in the body stops 'em. They drill a hole in you quicker'n anything. And if they hit a bone, they jist bust it apart. Lord, this thing's gonna hurt."

"But no bone."

"No."

"Got your madications ready?"

Before getting an answer, she pushed the visor up and looked over at the Russian again. His eyes had filled with tears, but his hands were steady on the wheel.

"Don't worry 'bout me, girl," came Bobbie Lee's voice, "I'll lit you know. But I might could do with some beer for the road."

CHAPTER 4

Lancaster County, August

As Coldgrave steered the Jaguar through the gateway and along the drive toward the Big House, she was glad that so much of it was behind her—the funeral, the project, the endless reports. Just outside the garage Bradley was hosing down the Corvette as she rounded the fountain and stopped by the entrance. Maggie would be there to greet her, Martina would not. In a way, she was glad Stanley would not be there, either. Following the funeral he had had an emotional breakdown and had returned to Moscow. Perhaps his return to Russia was for the best anyway, since the Agency had refused to allow him to continue with the team. They had also sharply criticized her decision to appoint him as team leader during the project's execution, although she had not been formally reprimanded. A tap on the windshield brought her back to herself, and she looked up through the glass to see Maggie's waving hand.

"I thought you were in a trance," said Maggie.

"So did I."

Together they extracted the heavy leather suitcase. Bradley, still holding the hose, called out to her and waved, saying he heard she was staying through the weekend. She returned the wave, but declined on calling back to him. Inside Maggie showed her to the guest room. After unpacking, she took a minute to look over her notes.

For dinner there was roast beef, potatoes, a variety of cooked vegetables garnered from a local farmers market. And of course, there was Maggie's own apple pie and homemade whipped cream. Coldgrave said she doubted whether she would fit in her swimsuit on Saturday. No one took her seriously. Then, with a glass of ice and gin in hand, she sat back to make a few announcements, which she warned might not be appreciated.

"First," she said, "I was asked to convey again the Agency's regret at the loss of dear Martina. With her superior success rate on the projects, she was considered to be the quintessential leader of an ad hoc team. She was a classy lady, an exemplary agent. She will be missed."

"All that was said at the funeral," said Gretchin, clinking her fork.

"Yes, but I have more to say, and they wanted me to say this first."

Maggie cleared her throat. "We will miss both of them. I loved Martina dearly, she was closer than a sister, much closer. And we all loved Stanley. We could go to him for everything, he seemed indispensable."

Bradley seemed clearly uncomfortable with this, but said nothing.

Coldgrave gave the ice in her glass a shake, then put the glass down and pushed it away from her. "I didn't tell you before, but the Agency simply said no. Since he had been an infiltrator, they said it would not be workable for him to stay even on the team. They were adamant, I'm afraid. By the way, he was given some money, a good sum actually, in appreciation for his services, and Martina's retirement from both her years of teaching and with the Agency will be his fully. She also had an insurance policy, which will go to him."

"Hooray," said Gretchin with a sardonic smile.

Coldgrave picked her glass up again and gave the ice another shake. "Would there perhaps be any more of the Sapphire, Maggie?" And with her glass soon replenished, she continued, "Since you have invited me to stay the weekend, I should just be up front about a few of the changes to the team. That way, we'll have plenty of time to discuss them. First off, as the Agency was not entirely happy with the way the Florida project was handled, by me I should say, although I was not officially reprimanded, it was suggested that I should go back into field service for a time. So, I have been appointed the new leader for this team. I hope this does not make any of you too unhappy."

There was a general silence, then Gretchin asked, "You'll be staying here?"

An affirming nod.

Connors, her tone clearly hostile, queried, "Joost what were they unhappy weth?"

"The way I handled things. They said the project had been carried out too noisily and cited the loss of Mrs. Osipov and the wounding of Ms. Henry."

Bobbie Lee offered wryly, "Yeah, I'll betcha they mintioned the noise first."

Coldgrave looked at her. "How is the leg?"

"I'm still usin' the crutches a little, and it still hurts, but it's not so bad on Jack Daniel's."

But Connors asked, "What was so noisy about et?"

"Well," said Coldgrave, "you did blow the front door in with shotguns in broad daylight in a residential area, kill the occupants in a horrific gunfight, and then burn the house down around their corpses. My superiors said it was a spectacle and embarrassing to the Agency."

"We were somewhat dasperate."

"You were angry, I think."

Connors' eyes narrowed. "No, we weren't angry, we were mad as goddamn fuckin' hell. And joost what en the fuckin' hell es wrong weth that?"

Dismissing this, "They said it was an embarrassment and could have been a disaster. We were lucky somebody from the fire department wasn't hurt by the stashed ammunition."

An audible smirk from Bobbie Lee. "It was Florida. I think it's a given that jist about ever'body in the South has ammo. The fire department knows that."

"I'm just giving you the Agency's assessment."

Connors replied, "And what was your assassmant, moight we ask?"

Coldgrave looked at her for a moment, then answered, "Actually they asked me that, too."

"And?"

"I told them I saw it your way."

Connors said nothing to this, but simply looked at her.

Then Maggie asked softly, "What exactly will be done about the woman on the beach who made the call?"

With a sympathetic look, "After her direct role in Martina's murder the Agency saw her as a viable accomplice, so it has been taken care of. Let's just say, she now sleeps with the fishes, or rather, turtles, since that is apropos."

Maggie looked down. "Good."

Just before ten the next morning Gretchin spread a rose-and-black blanket beside the pool and lay down to enjoy the serenity. Between projects the pool had become for her a diversion from the mentality of the work, and the fact that such work had at times been mind crippling for her, made the diversion a nearly indispensable amenity. Often she found herself alone there, sleeping or reading away a morning or an afternoon on a blanket beneath one of the white umbrellas. At such times, her harsh world seemed to change into a paradise. Now, her eyes closed and her breathing eased, she was brought to herself only by Maggie's voice.

"I've brought you something, if you're awake."

After placing on the blanket a glass of lemonade and pressing it into the cloth to steady it, Maggie sat down and crossed her legs. Nearby the powerful German Shepherd Helga and the ferocious Jindo-Chow Tai Ping, tired from prowling the perimeter of the property, lay dosing in the sun, as if to recharge their batteries. Donning sunglasses, she sighed with pleasure as she looked into the depths of the water.

"Thanks," said Gretchin, sitting up to give the drink a taste. "Nothing in it, I take it?"

"Not a thing, just a good dose of lemon and pure, unadulterated processed sugar. You'll love it."

Momentarily, "You miss her like crazy, don't you?"

"She was a part of me, what can I say? Her absence is like the absence of light. It's ironic that she's the one who used to pretend she was blind. Now I feel blind without her."

"Is Mary coming out? I suppose she's sleeping late?"

Maggie sighed. "I just saw her. She'll be out in a minute or so, I should think."

"Should I expect something dramatic, like a thousand-dollar bathing suit? Or maybe that would be cheap for her."

"I'd say, about four or five thousand. But then, she won't know, will she?"

Raising the glass to her lips, Gretchin fixed her gaze upon the door. Then it opened and Coldgrave emerged. Wearing a wide-brimmed straw hat, a revealing and obviously expensive green swimsuit, and silver pool slippers, she walked toward them, a bright yellow towel over an arm.

"Hello, good morning," she said to them. "My, you two are up early."

Silently they watched as she spread the blanket and sat down. Then Gretchin returned, "It's not early, it's ten thirty, Mary."

"Yes, well, early birds and all that, I would say. And look at that water. It's splendid, like a big glass of gin. I would love this, or I guess I will, for sure."

"Right," returned Maggie, with an indescreet roll of her eyes. "It's not a large pool, but it's nice."

"Like a bathtub. But yes, so nice. I love it, I do."

"You're probably used to something larger."

"Not too. But somewhat, yes. This is cute though—cozy, I should say."

"And when will you be moving in, do you think?"

"As soon as a few minor changes can be made to the Osipov's old room. It is delightful here, I cannot wait."

Then a silence fell upon them, an awkward silence, until at last Maggie broke it. "Mary, could I ask you something?"

"Surely, anything you like, that's why I'm here."

"I don't mean as team leader, I mean on a personal level."

"Surely."

"How old were you when you became aware that your family was—rich?"

Thoughtfully, "That's difficult to say. Maybe after I had my first drink. Does that sound right?"

"And—that would have been?"

"Not sure, really. Perhaps when I was eight or six—no, maybe younger."

"So," said Gretchin, "you actually knew then that you were rich, or at least that your family was?"

"Sort of, yes."

Gretchin gave her nose a scratch. "Were you ever called—a snob?"

Somewhat astonished, "I? I don't think so."

"You played with other rich children?"

"I'm not sure. I mean, I suppose they were rich. I do remember though that some of them didn't like to drink. Isn't that amazing?"

"Uh-huh."

Maggie smiled. "But you did."

"Of course. I loved everything that was delicious. Still do."

"Your first drink was a mixed drink, I take it."

"Possibly, yes. But I do remember my first taste of gin. That, of course, was straight. I was eight, and it was at a Christmas party. Or was it Halloween? Well, I don't exactly remember that part, but it was definitely a party. I poured myself a little glass from a bottle of ice-cold gin. I forget the brand—isn't that amazing? But I do remember that it was incredibly delicious. My father saw me and said that I was not allowed a second."

"You thought it was delicious?"

"Oh yes. Still do."

"You didn't have to get used to it at all?"

"No. What's to get used to?"

"Did it affect you?"

"Not really, no."

"And if your father hadn't said anything, you would have poured a second drink?"

"Probably, yes. There was a lot of it around, you understand."

"Of course," Maggie returned. And giving Gretchin a nod, "Yes, that makes perfect sense."

And Gretchin, nodding back, chimed, "Perfect sense, yes."

But just then Packard, coming from the house, called, "Hey, ladies, mind if I take a dip? Don't mean to disturb you." But when Maggie gestured for him to go ahead, he chuckled, sat down, slipped into the water, and swam toward them. "I had some of your lemonade, Mags. It needs something, I don't know what."

"Right," she returned wryly. "Don't tell me, vodka?"

"That might do the trick, yep."

Coldgrave brightened. "I had some of Maggie's excellent lemonade for breakfast, Mr. Packard, and I did add a little vodka to mine. I wouldn't say it improved the lemonade, but it did seem to improve me."

CHAPTER 5

On the day Coldgrave came to stay she parked the Jaguar next to the Corvette and moved into what had been the Osipovs' room. A moving company had been secured to deliver her clothes and other things. Maggie and Gretchin volunteered to help with the wardrobe.

"I just want to thank everyone," Coldgrave said following dinner that evening, "for all your excellent help and for welcoming me to the team and making me feel at home here at the Estate. I guess this can be our first meeting, and well, any questions?"

"I've got one," said Gretchin, "who the hell's our new contact?"

With a shake of her head, "I have no idea, sorry."

"So, no new project yet?"

"No, the Agency tries pretty much to stick to the structure, so until they appoint a contact, they won't give us a project. Maybe in an emergency, yes, but otherwise we won't hear anything unless it's through the new person."

Bradley, who had been staring at her, looked away. Reaching for her glass, she recalled he had nearly oggled her the day of her first swim in the pool. It had been obvious that whatl he really wanted was for her simply to take the suit off and swim around a little for him. But with Gretchin watching him, he had suddenly looked away then too. A lot of people are like that, she thought, tipping up the glass—they are interested in you for only as long as it seems feasible that you might fulfill their desires. They don't want to fulfill yours, of course, but only and always only theirs.

"More of the porter, Mary?" asked Maggie.

"No, Maggie, thanks," she replied, throwing a glance in Bradley's direction. "I'll make this do for now."

Over the next few weeks Coldgrave worked with the team to refresh her skills with their preferred handguns. With each team member, who pretended to be wounded, she practiced taking up their gun or getting it from its holster, firing until it was empty, then reloading it and firing again. She even took a turn at pulling both of Packard's seven-shot magnums from the jackass rig as he lay prone as if wounded, and with one in each hand, throwing all fourteen shots downrange, then reloading from his pocketed speed-loaders and firing again.

Her go-to person for all of this was Packard. On weekday mornings, following a light breakfast, she would carry her bag to the range, don hearing protectors in the safety zone, and march into the shooting area. He was usually there already to clear the brass and turn on the exhaust fans. On the occasions when she arrived after ten, he would grumble out that sleeping in was for rich people, not for people who got things done.

Since joining the Agency she had enjoyed the study of weapons. She had not been allowed to play with guns as a child, which she complained of as being very strange, since every little girl, she said, should be able to protect her dolls and her dog from monsters. As an agent she had immersed herself in the subject of guns, learning everything she could about the spectrum ranging from WWI weapons to the modern. By the time she was appointed as team contact, she was recognized by Agency authorities as a small-arms expert.

Her personal gun was a Smith 642 five-shot .38 special, usually carried loose in her purse or coat pocket. She had no intention of changing up to one of the popular semi-autos, since for her, reliability always trumped capacity. The smooth white bone grips rendered it, to her mind, a charming piece, and when Packard joked that she might consider going bigger with one of his 686es, she simply said she did not wish to trade a beauty for a beast.

"At least get two of them," he growled once after she had emptied the gun downrange, drilling the red at forty feet. "Sure you're good, but you can run out pretty quick."

"One's enough," she replied. "Besides, where would I hide another? But I do want to add one piece to my little arsenal, just as a back-up, you understand, a short 12 pump. I might need to get through a door sometime. And I want slugs and triple-aught."

"That ain't a back-up," he retorted, "that's a battering ram. A slug will knock a man down, all right, even kill him, but triple-aught will blow his goddamn head off. You've got a mean streak, lady."

But his grin told her he was pleased, as only an old killer can be, and she told him she was ordering it with a walnut stock and a rubber butt. Then he let his gaze fall and walked away, muttering that it was going to be great. She watched him, this old angelic form of a devil, as he grabbed the broom to sweep up the brass, the warmth in her stomach practically aglow. But if familiar with such joys, she was also familiar with the opposite, and as he stooped there, black metal dustpan in hand, like an old-school soldier, she recalled how he and Bradley, supposedly out of earshot, had joked that if she used to give them an erection when she walked, she didn't anymore.

As fall approached she was still able to swim with Gretchin and Maggie. Hour upon hour they spent under the umbrellas, sipping lemonade laced with vodka. Their acceptance of her was so close to perfect that she became dubious about leading them, for it was a given, especially after Florida, that the Agency would be ramping up the danger level of the projects.

Toward the end of September, after Connors and Bobbie Lee had returned from a short camping trip on the Harley, Coldgrave heard from the Agency. It was the new contact himself who called. Three days later he arrived in an Agency-looking sedan and with an Agency-looking sidekick.

"Hi," he said as he faced the team, his expression painfully amiable, "I'm Bob, last name Willard, as Mrs. Swift-Jones Packard has said, and I am your new contact person for the projects you will be assigned."

Oh my, thought Maggie, another Kessler. God help us when Gretchin gets at him, for she will be merciless.

"I should let you know that Ms. Coldgrave and I know each other from the New York office. We worked together for a number of years and are quite familiar with each other's quirks—ha. Just let me sit down here and we'll begin. Oh, and this is George. Say hi, George."

With this, he sat beside George and smiled broadly upon them all, as a pastor would upon his congregation. Secretly he tried to calm himself. Individually and collectively they made him nervous. Like a kind of menagerie of misfits, they gave him the creeps. He became convinced that in order to deal with them calmly and keep his self-respect, he must do a bit of playacting. Casting a glance at the huge dog eyeing him from his stuffed chair, he continued, "Now, you're all familiar with the roll of a team's contact person, so I won't go into it. . . . Are there any questions you might have for me?"

Gretchin wrinkled her nose, as if she had smelled a bad odor. Giving his bland sweater and khakis a once-over, she replied, "So, you're going to treat us like kids, huh?"

He stared at her. "I, uh, I should hope not, Ms. Wheeler."

"That would be good. I know I sure as hell would take a piss on the carpet, if you did."

Another, colder stare. "Okay, well," he said timorously, "I'll keep that in mind, I will." Then, blinking, he said weakly to them all, "Don't be shy, I'll listen to anything you have to say. Just be blunt, if you will."

Coldgrave watched his eyes fall upon Connors and Bobbie Lee and his expression grow visibly more timorous. "Maybe," she offered, "there is news about the projects. Is there a new one for us, Bob?"

"Yes," he replied happily. "Yes, there is, thank you, Mary. I do have a new project, yes, and I can assure you all that with its completion this team will have done the world a great service."

"Oh God," said Gretchin, "not another crockful of moralistic thick stuff."

Even again he stared, then continued, as if she had not spoken, "We have identified a somewhat serious threat to a school in western Ukraine. We do not want to see that area destabilized any further, of course, so the Agency has determined that the threat must be eliminated. The hitch is, and this is why we're using our people instead of turning the whole thing over to the Ukrainians, the threat is coming from someone here. Long story short, your targets will be two men and a woman living in a rented house in a Pennsylvania state park called Black Moshannon. Does anyone know the place?"

"Good Lord," said Bobbie Lee, "me 'n Killy here were jist there with the bike campin'. This is weird."

"Well then, you two know the area, which will be useful, I'm sure."

"Et moight be a hendrance too," said Connors. "The motorcycle's pretty loud, they moight've seen us."

"Think they would recognize either of you? If they get suspicious and run, we're in trouble."

"Don't t'ink so, we had halmets on whan we rode. We ded a lot of walkin', but wore hats."

"We should be okay, then. Anyway, a quite viable problem is that our window is limited, very limited. We have two weeks to get them before their rental runs out."

"Gits cold up there," said Bobbie Lee. "They said the lake freezes hard by Halloween."

"Ms. Henry, what does that have to do with anything?"

"Jist sayin'."

"Right, okay. Oh, and they're working from their phones, so you must recover their phones, including any you can find in the house. They're probably only using three, but get them. If we can't crack them, at least we'll have them. Fortunately we have some intel. The three of them make a trip into the nearest town, at the bottom of the mountain, nearly every Saturday. If you can hit them outside the park, that would be ideal. It could be really dirty inside the park, but even if you have to do it there, get them. We're putting you right into the park, into one of their modern cabins, so you'll be comfortable and can keep tabs on them.

You'll need to take bed linens and a few things, but it won't be for long. And when you finish, get out quietly. We don't want to disturb the wood-chucks."

"Are these people armed?" queried Gretchin.

"Yes, they are, but not heavily. Nothing like the Florida couple, not even close. As far as we know, just a few handguns. You should be okay. . . . Oh, and feel free to be creative, but maybe not as creative as in Florida."

Connors looked at him. "We got tham for yous, dedn't we?"

"Yeah," he replied, nodding, "but the aftermath was a little dirty for us to vacuum up. There was a lot of clutter. Try to keep the clutter down, if you can, that's all I'm saying."

"What's the matter," she returned, "yous don't loike foires?"

He looked at her. God, what a beautiful woman, he thought, and yet what a mess too. And what's with the spooky eyes? She looks demonic. Why'd we hire this woman anyway? The file said she's been shot numerous times, even carries bullet fragments in her. Carries a five-shot in a flash bra—unbelievable. She looks like a nut, has to have a screw loose. Then he replied soberly, "Just try not to burn the house down this time, okay? It's a state park, it wouldn't be good."

She flinched, but then returned the gravity by sending him a hard, unforgiving look. "Don't wet yersalf, Bob. We'll gat your fuckin' phones for yous."

Instantly he felt embarassed, as if she had slapped him across the mouth. Taking just a moment to regain his composure, he noticed that Coldgrave was watching him for a reaction, which made him feel even more embarassed. He had never liked her, this lush, at least since discovering she was pretty much an alcoholic, and more than once he had shown his disdain for her, if only in a petty way. So, here he was, appointed as her replacement, doing a really stinky job while she watched him for his reaction to an overt insult from a godforsaken killer. But she couldn't blame him for being uncertain and perhaps being over-cautious here, for with Connors one was practically dealing with the Devil.

Finally he replied simply, "Thank you, Ms. Connors." But her hard look was still there, and he nearly gulped when she told him not to fucking mention it.

CHAPTER 6

Black Moshannon State Park, Early October

From the SUV's cargo bay Connors, Bobbie Lee, and Bradley continued extracting luggage, linens, food box, and cooler, and carrying them into the cabin, where Gretchin was putting things away and preparing to make up the beds. They repeated the action for the weapons cases, while Coldgrave watched from the doorway.

"Not used to this, I guess," said Bobbie Lee, uncapping a bottle of spring water and handing it to her. "Rich people don't know what life on the other side of town's like, do they? Well, look at it this way, you're gittin' a valuable experience."

"Oh, I'm sure I am," replied Coldgrave, taking a sip from the bottle, as if to show she didn't need a cup. "I always enjoy a stretch of the mind. This is rustic, it's camping, isn't it?"

"Not quite."

"But we're here, and it's cute, quaint. The water's quite tasty, but would you have anything else?"

"Gotta leave the park for that. It's illegal here."

Coldgrave smiled. "Oh, that's fine, it doesn't really matter."

"State parks are usually dry. Ever been to one before?"

"Perhaps," replied Coldgrave, taking another sip.

"Well, you gotta watch your P's 'n Q's or the ranger will definitely git you."

"And what then?"

"He'll kick you out, maybe even fine you."

"You know this by experience?"

"I'm not a miscreant, Mary."

"I'm sure you're not. And you aren't, either, are you, Kelly?"

Connors opened one of the bottles, took a sip, then recapped it and said, "There's a bar not far from the park. Lat's all take a droive."

"A rustic bar?" asked Coldgrave. "Does that mean with trucks?"

The bar, indeed rustic, and therefore suitable for hunters and campers not willing to risk being caught with alcohol inside the park, seemed to slouch like an old cardboard box in the pale twilight. As the SUV entered the gravel lot, Coldgrave commented that it did not appear to be a suitable place to find refreshment. Bradley held the door open as they walked under a weathered pair of mounted antlers and entered the establishment.

It was a small place, with space only for its bar, five tables, a jukebox, and an area where two or three couples could dance. Four men with hunting caps sat at a table close to the bar. As the five took a corner table the denim-aproned bartender sauntered over.

"You people look like you're from somewhere else," he offered jovially, wiping his hands on the apron. "What can I get you? The kitchen's closed." But eyeing Coldgrave's leather-trimmed tweed cloak, he added, "My wife can make you a sandwich, if you want."

Bradley put a hand up. "I'll have a draught beer, if you have it, preferably lager. How about you girls?"

They deemed it wise to keep the orders simple, and soon they settled in with drinks and a large bowl of pretzels. More people arrived, both men and women, until all the tables were taken. Soon the room was filled with low laughter and carefree chatter.

"How's the Jack?" queried Bradley, his eyes on Bobbie Lee's glass.

"It's a-workin'," she returned. "How's the beer, bubba?"

"A little warm. Cold beer is always better." Then he said to Coldgrave, "And is the ice clear enough for our team leader?"

Peering into her glass, "Perhaps I should not be particular."

"You strike me as being someone who's used to being particular."

She drew her breath slowly, and her eye rested upon him. Lifting the glass, she took in more of the iced gin. What was it with this guy? What exactly, outside of a car, a gun, a flag, a mechanism or symbol of some kind, made his computer run? What exactly made him favor some things or target others? Just why, as she sat there quietly enduring his homey bar, had he targeted her? Practically in seconds she counted down to the moment he would now speak.

As he met her eye he said, "If you took your shooting gloves off, you'd look less conspicuous."

She looked at him, as if to consider a specimen. There it was, his ploy, his pretentious wedge in the door, that would allow him eventually to shout through the crack and into her room his opinion that he found her to be distasteful. He wouldn't mind having her, but since he couldn't, he would instead simply find her to be loathsome. But life was like that, she thought. It did not merely give you your reality to deal with, it gave you the opinions of other people to deal with.

"Yes," she returned, "I could take them off, and then I would look less conspicuous, like you, Bradley. You are definitely not conspicuous."

Scowling, "What's that supposed to mean?"

With a chuckle, Gretchin said to him, "That you lack distinction, sophistication, maybe?"

"Well, is that so great, being sophisticated? Maybe I don't want to be sophisticated, maybe I just want to be regular. This isn't New York, you know, it's just a normal, regular place."

Ignoring him, Coldgrave raised a gloved hand to the bartender for service. After ordering a scotch on the rocks, she crossed her legs and looked out over the patrons, all as if Bradley was not at the table.

He eyed her for this, but said nothing more until she had tasted the drink.

"So, Mary, are you saying I'm not cool like your rich friends? What's the word, *elite*?" When still she did not answer, he said, "Come on, I don't care what you think, say what you want." And when she still did not respond, he said, "You think you're elite, don't you?"

Connors and Bobbie Lee, who had long tired of the seemingly endless bickering between him and Gretchin, said nothing to interrupt the stream of this new entertainment. It was as if someone had flipped the channel. Bobbie Lee gave her Jack Daniel's a swirl and threw Connors a grin.

"Well, don't you, Mary?" he persisted, taking another pull at his beer. "Look at the clothes and everything. Every single thing you wear costs about a zillion dollars. And how about the Jag, tell me that's not elite." And to Gretchin, "That's hoity-toity, right? A Corvette's just fast and cool, but a Jaguar's elite, right?"

Reaching for a pretzel, Gretchin replied, "Careful, big guy, you can't play chess, and she won't play checkers."

"*She*?" he snickered contemptuously. "She's so rich and considers herself to be so special, she might as well be a he—at least, to me and maybe to other men. I mean, talk about being on a pedestal."

Calmly, Coldgrave set the empty glass down, motioned for the bartender again, then said, "Bradley, you are being quite judgmental, nearly offensively so, and your comments are abject at best."

"Yeah, but see that, look at that right there. What's that supposed to mean, *abject?* I'll bet you nobody in this room knows what that means, except you. So, you're being elite again, which is what I said."

Gretchin, now clearly annoyed, said to him, "She's not being elite, Bradley. She's simply trying to deal with someone whom she has to work with, yet who always makes himself the biggest goddamn prick in the room."

But he glared at her and retorted, "I'm just saying she's proud, Gretchin, that's all. That's my point."

"Yeah, well, I'm not sure you're capable of making a point, Bradley. At least, not an intelligent one."

Now he reddened. "Well, I'm saying she's proud and the gloves make her look like it. Or maybe I should say *him*, they make *him* look like it." And he turned his head away in anger.

Coldgrave lifted the empty glass, sniffed it, then said, "You can say *him*, if you like, Bradley, and you can say I'm rich and proud. I don't really care what you think of me or call me. There's no life rule that says people have to like each other. You're entitled to think of me as you wish."

But he glared at her for this, and then at Gretchin, and told them both to just leave him alone. Jerking his chair sideways, he turned away from them to watch an older couple, who had taken to the dance floor and were moving to a Brenda Lee song from the sixties.

Then Connors, leaning into Bobbie Lee, said, although not inaudibly, "Jerk!"

"You said it, girl. He's pathetic. I think we gotta git him another man to talk football with or somethin'. Jist bein' around us seems to make him nasty."

After retrieving her charger, Bobbie Lee locked the SUV down for the night. At the cabin door she turned to note the lights of the park ranger's jeep as he made his eleven o'clock rounds.

If Bradley and Coldgrave avoided each other following their words in the bar, Connors and Bobbie Lee each seemed to seek personal space for positive reasons. Even Gretchin found a corner, where she could let her mind go dead playing Freecell solitaire. The fact was that on the next day, Friday, they would all need to be engaged with surveillance and preparation, since Saturday was the day they must act. But after an hour or so of down time, they gathered at Coldgrave's summons around the kitchen table.

"One day left," she said, "one day for watching them and preparing for Saturday. Note possible snags and blind spots and try to do a mental workaround on the spot. Above all, make it all come together in your own mind, especially taking into account what might go wrong. Our window is limited, Saturday must be the day for everything to be executed, no matter how badly it goes. . . . Thoughts?"

"Well," said Gretchin, "I'm not sleeping with him tonight, Florida was bad enough. So, how're we doing the three bedrooms?"

"I meant about tomorrow, any thoughts about that?"

Bradley straightened himself. "I don't want to sleep with you, either, Gretchin."

"Please, people," remonstrated Coldgrave, "the project first, okay?"

"What's to think 'bout?" said Bobbie Lee. "We all know what we're s'pposed to do. Lit's jist do it, that's all."

And after no one else spoke, Coldgrave said, "All right, about the rooms, Bradley can take a double for himself, then Kelly and Bobbie Lee the other one, and Gretchin and I will take the two singles in the last. Is that all right with everyone?"

"Suits me," said Bradley, "I'd rather be by myself." His eyes went around the table, resting upon Coldgrave, who still wore the gloves. A chill went through him at the thought of having to sleep with her. But any configuration was possible on the projects, considering cover, strategy, accommodations. He made a mental note to foresee any such an arrangement and avoid it.

"And," she added, "let's try not to aggravate each other about the single bathroom. Bob said he had to go with this place, as the other cabins had been taken. . . . All right, let's get some sleep. Breakfast is at seven. Bobbie Lee, Gretchin, can you have things ready for that? And then back here for lunch. See you all tomorrow."

CHAPTER 7

If ducks and birds called to each other as the sun climbed, the rest of the animal life of Black Moshannon's preserved natural habitats seemed reticent, as though aware that within a few short weeks fishermen would be cracking the lake ice for fishing while snowmobiles whined along through the woods. That's the way it had been since the lakes were formed when the trees were cut and the streams were dammed up. Called Moshannon, meaning moose crossing, by Native Americans long before, and deemed Black for its tea-colored water, the area exuded the sweet odors of decaying timber and both stagnant and flowing water.

Not much seemed to be moving across the green and lavender landscape as Bobbie Lee and Connors made their way past the targets' house. It was cold, and they could see their breath as they talked. There seemed to be no activity inside or outside the house. A hundred yards behind, Coldgrave followed, all as if out for a morning stroll. Both parties noted that the faded-green minivan was parked beside the porch just as intel had reported. When Bobbie Lee pointed out a fat woodchuck ambling close to the marshes beside the macadam roadway, Connors giggled at the sight, something she did not often do, but then looked over her shoulder to catch the tweeds of Coldgrave, who was just then passing the house.

Out on the highway Bradley and Gretchin drove to the town, where they were to fill the SUV's tank, then return along the same route, carefully noting the curves, dips, and width variations of the roadway. Oddly, they found nothing to argue about.

At lunch Coldgrave reported that on her return walk she had gotten a positive on the woman. Bobbie Lee and Connors reported likewise on the men. When they had finished the lunch, Coldgrave went outside and called Willard.

"All right," she said, returning to the table, "it's a go for tomorrow. Now, my dear colleagues— scenarios, let's hear them, please. . . . Oh, and I was thinking we might want to go again to that little tavern this evening, just for a nightcap, you understand. As you know, I always drink in moderation. It is chilly out and something to keep us warm would be good, don't you think?"

"Let's get there while the kitchen's open and try dinner this time," suggested Bobbie Lee. "I want to put a different sleeve on the P-64's grip, and it would help me not to have to think about gittin' ever'body's dinner."

The tavern was dark when they entered at just after six, except for the neon beer signs shining from behind the bar. Two men were on stools at the bar, and another table was occupied. This time the bartender brought menus.

"Order anything you like," he said, "it's Friday night and the kitchen's open. And what's everybody want to drink?"

An hour later Bobbie Lee grabbed her beer glass and sat back, a look of satisfaction on her face. "Now, wasn't that great?" she said. "What's better'n a hamburger and beer, tell me what?"

"Except," retorted Bradley, "that Mary here looks a little green."

Coldgrave offered a noncommittal smile. "Actually, I have been to a barbecue before, so I knew what to expect, and yes, Ms. Henry, this dinner wasn't that bad at all." And lifting her glass, "I feel nearly refreshed, honestly."

"Right, sure," said Bradley with a chuckle. "Well, at least they had your gin, that's pretty good."

Gretchin put her glass down. "The Bombay's acceptable for you, Mary?"

"Of course," answered Coldgrave, pulling her gloves on. "Quite acceptable."

She felt it odd that such a strong feeling of camaraderie should be coming over her, and as she looked around at them her heart grew both warm with love and cold with fear. Perhaps these were the emotions Martina had felt. Even Bradley seemed friendlier as he sat there grinning at her. Before, when she had viewed him merely to be a fool, he was only tolerable, but now somehow he was almost acceptable, like family.

"So," he queried, still grinning, "how about the expensive stuff though? You probably drink really good gin when you're in New York. How much does that cost?"

Gretchin put a hand to her forehead. "Don't be a dick, Bradley. Try to fake a little class, please."

But Coldgrave replied, "I have no idea, Bradley, any more than how much my car or shoes or anything else costs. What's the difference?"

He groaned. "I think there's a lot of difference between a car and a pair of shoes."

"But I don't."

His brow furrowing, "Well, maybe you should."

"In what way, would you say, morally or ideally?"

"Yes, right, sure," he stammered.

"Which?"

"Okay, morally."

"Please explain."

"It's not right," he said, "to value a car, especially a Jaguar, which is a famous car, like it was just a pair of shoes."

"But I do, Bradley," she replied simply, "I do."

Gretchin reached for her beer. "Be careful, Bradley. You'd better put your Bible down, pal, or I might just spread a few facts on the table to show why you shouldn't be thumping it."

"Hey, this is gittin' fun," said Bobbie Lee to Bradley. "You keep comin' back for more. But I will say this, you're playin' a bad hand, bubba. Only dummies will play a hand as bad as you're holdin'. Besides, I'd like to strut myself up and down naked in a pair of Mary's shoes. From what I hear, some of them are probably worth more'n a car."

Then she and Connors laughed and Coldgrave flashed them a classy smile, but Bradley dismissed them all with a wave, declaring they were crazy.

Later, after plans were made to deal with various scenarios for the next day and they had all gone to bed, Gretchin went to Bradley's room. Closing the door behind her, she leaned against it and looked at him for a moment.

"What's your problem with her?" she asked.

Simply, "I don't like rich people."

With a labored sigh, "What's the problem?"

"*And*, I despise alcoholics."

"Oh, Bradley. Really?"

He jammed the .45 home into its center-of-the-back holster and laid the rig down. "Maybe it doesn't bother you, but it bothers me. Who am I following into the thing tomorrow, or on any of the other projects—a drunk?"

"We haven't seen her drunk. Competency matters, right?"

"Yeah, sure it does. But there's also attitude and potential failure. She's got a richy's attitude, and she could easily fail because of the alcohol. So, I don't trust her, not one bit." He followed this with a quick shrug, then sat down upon the bed.

"Those are pathetic reasons. Some people might think that you've got a thing for her, and that you made advances, but she turned you down."

"Garbage."

"It does happen, Bradley."

"Garbage."

"Well, you've screwed me more than once."

"Don't talk like that."

"She's beautiful."

"So?"

"So, you keep picking on her, like you're thowing pebbles at her window or something."

Momentarily, "I don't like you telling me what's wrong with me. I don't want to hear it, not from you. Talk about picking on someone, you've picked on me since I've known you."

Ignoring this, she said, "You wanted to be team leader when we were still an advisory team. When we were made agents, you hated having Stanley, as a Russian, invited to join us. When Martina was killed and Mary appointed him instead of you as temporary team leader, it made you mad as hell. And then, to have Mary be appointed team leader and then show up at the pool in a sensuous swimsuit, well, that fried your circuits, didn't it?"

"That's your opinion."

"You saw her shoot. Packard saw her shoot. He says she's great. When she walked onto that range and pulled that .38 fast as anything and blazed away and put them all in the black—I mean, Jesus, Bradley, my mouth fell open. Besides that, she's a walking encyclopedia of firearms. And besides all that, she tries to be fair with the team."

Folding his arms, he simply looked at her.

"Look," she said, "You need to get over your problem with her, because the rest of us are on her side."

"So, why don't you get out of my room. Tomorrow I have to both drive the car and maybe shoot somebody."

"You'd better deal with this," she said, opening the door, "because the rest of us like her, and we like her a lot."

Pulling the door shut, she watched as Coldgrave in a sumptuous pink robe exited the bathroom and came toward her. Closing her eyes for a moment, she wondered how anyone with that much alcohol in her could still be walking around, let alone walking straight.

Coldgrave stopped and smiled. "Having a talk with Mr. Hopkins?"

"Yes."

"To any avail?"

"I doubt it."

"Well, come to bed when you like, you won't disturb me. Try to sleep, if you can."

"I will."

CHAPTER 8

Everyone arose at five. Following a quick breakfast, they worked as a unit to remove the bed
linens, pack up, and load the SUV. At just before
six, they sat in the kitchen to give weapons and
ammunition a final check, while Coldgrave gave a
brief recap of the proposed scenarios. Finishing,
she dropped the cabin keys into the center of the
table and threw her cloak around her shoulders.

With Bobbie Lee in the navigator's seat,
Coldgrave behind her, Connors in the middle, then
Gretchin behind him, Bradley eased the SUV out
onto the frosty macadam that led to the lake. Two
semiauto 12 gauges had been placed, in opposite
directions, across the rear floor at the feet of the
three women. Within minutes Bradley had made
the final turn to bring them onto the road beside
the lake. Slowly they rolled past the house.

"All right," said Coldgrave, "their car's there, so
they're probably getting ready to leave, if of course
they are going to leave. Intel said they leave around

seven, so let's bet they do the same today. Turn around up here on your left, Bradley, take us back to the dock area, and then back us in."

"Of course," he returned, "as planned. I do know the plan, Mary."

"I'm sure you do, Mr. Hopkins."

After backing them off the road, he let the engine idle and checked again the .45 riding at the center of his back. Gretchin and Coldgrave got out and began walking back down the road toward the house. All seemed quiet on the lake. Gretchin checked her watch. There was no activity at the house as they passed. Then the two men emerged, got into the car, backed it down the drive, and drove toward the dock area. As the two women continued to walk Coldgrave opened her phone and called Bobbie Lee.

"Just the two men are in the car," she said in a low voice. "They're yours, we'll take the woman. Remember, only texting now."

Then she let the phone fall back into the pocket of the cloak. As their eyes met they turned and began walking back toward the house.

"Well," said Gretchin, "at least Kelly won't be burning the house down."

At the border of the park, the faded-green car turned onto the highway that led to the town. Soon the SUV did the same.

"Look at all the campers," remarked Bradley, noting the many cars coming at him in the other lane, some with canoes or kayaks on top or bikes at the rear. "I wouldn't want to be trying to find a campsite on Saturday morning."

Bobbie Lee agreed, checking the 19 and the speed-loaders. "You're right, to git a good site you gotta git there at least by Friday night." And holding the gun in front of her, "I love this gun. Combat Magnum, in blue, look at that, talk about a classic."

Glancing over, he said, "So, you sleep with that?"

"I do."

Momentarily, his hand shifted on the wheel. "Okay, I think that's them—yep. All right, the road looks pretty clear behind us. Let's wait for the oncoming traffic to clear out. Goofy campers."

"*I'm* a camper, bubba."

When they were a hundred feet behind the car, Bobbie Lee popped off her seatbelt and turned slightly toward her window. Connors moved over directly behind Bradley, put her back against the door, then lifted one of the shotguns, flipped its safety off, and let it rest on her leg.

For a few moments, they did not say anything, surrounded by only the eerie, muffled road noise as the SUV's tires rolled over the highway and its hulk moved through the air. Then, touching his panel and lowering the right-side windows, Bradley said, "All right, this is it, here we go." Slowly he moved them forward, but then suddenly he accelerated and moved them into the oncoming lane, as if to pass the car.

When they were beside the car, simultaneously Connors lunged forward with the shotgun and shoved its barrel out the window and toward the driver's head, and Bobbie Lee stuck the magnum out her window and aimed at the passenger's head.

Then both opened fire and continued firing until the guns were empty. The hugely explosive blasting by the Smith and the shotgun sprayed glass not only inward at the targets but back into the SUV, while the residue fragments were blown away by the rushing air. Instantly Bradley decelerated and pulled them up behind the still-moving car.

Rapidly the car slowed and began to veer right, until after another few hundred feet it left the roadway and cluncked wretchedly into the trees. Bradley pulled to the shoulder, where both women got out. Bobbie Lee drew the P-64 from her back holster, while Connors extracted the .38 from her jacket pocket. But there was no movement in the car. As they looked through the blown-in window they saw that much of the driver's head had been blasted away by the buckshot and seemed now to be attached to the neck by gruesome strands of shredded meat. The other corpse, supported by the seatbelt's shoulder strap, was an oozing heap, with one hole in the cheek and one in the neck, and with the left eye completely shot out.

"Whew," said Bobbie Lee, "what a Jesus mess, look at that. Think I'll turn vegetarian."

But Connors, pocketing the .38 and pulling the door open, said, "Lat's gat the phones. I'll gat thes one, you gat the other."

Reholstering, Bobbie Lee went to the other side, lifted the button and gave the handle a pull. "Ah shit, it's like a butcher shop."

"Joost gat the phones."

"Shewy, this thing's gonna stink like a meat dumpster here pritty soon."

Returning to the SUV, they dropped the phones into a plastic bag and cleaned their hands with wipes. As Bradley moved them from the shoulder and back onto the highway, a car loaded with gear and bicycles was already slowing to have a look at the wreckage.

"That was some show," said Bradley, now looking for a place to make a U-turn. "It was like two machine guns."

"Yeah, well," said Bobbie Lee, flipping the mirror down, "I've got glass in my hair from it. And you should've seen it in the car. Killy nearly blew the bastard's head off. That car's gonna stink pritty soon." Then she picked up the Smith, ejected the spent cartridges onto the floor, and fitted a speed-loader to the cylinder.

"Hey, watch the carpet," he whined.

"Don't worry 'bout it," she returned, "it looks a whole lot better than theirs."

Even as this part of the attack had been transpiring Gretchin and Coldgrave were making their approach to the house. As they climbed the old wooden steps to the front porch Coldgrave put her hand into her cloak pocket and closed upon the .38. Gretchin looked at her, then knocked upon the screen door. In a moment the inside door was pulled open and the woman stood at the screen.

"Yes?" she said.

Gretchin smiled. "We're just looking for a rental. Isn't there a house for rent around here? We've been looking for the sign, but can't find it."

At first the woman hesitated, but then replied, "No, not that I know of. We're renting this one, and we'll be out soon. You would have to talk to the realtor to see if it's available." But then, for some reason, she put her hand on the inside door to begin closing it.

As deftly as a dog would lift its paw Coldgrave pulled the .38, leveled it, and fired three times through the screen—*Blat! Blat! Blat!* The door held fast as Gretchin then yanked at it, so she rammed her fist through the bullet-torn screen and felt frantically for the latch. The woman, now on the floor, was moaning and wiping the saliva from her mouth. She began to weep loudly as Gretchin lifted the latch and opened the door. Coldgrave stepped inside, fired while standing into the woman's chest, then stooped, put the muzzle to the forehead, and fired again.

After dragging the legs free, they closed the door and searched the house for cell phones. They found only one. Pulling the inside door closed and letting the screen door seat quietly, they left the porch and headed for the roadway. Before crossing the macadam, they waited for a car laden with camping equipment to pass. Leisurely they began to walk back toward the dock area. Gretchin retrieved her phone and texted Bradley, *Success. Ready to meet.* Moments later the phone vibrated, and she read, *Success. On our way.*

At the rendezvous point they sat down on a park bench and looked out over the placid water.

Gretchin, checking her phone for the time, said, "That was some pretty cool shooting back there."

Casually, "Oh well, yes. It could have gone badly, but it didn't."

"Well, I was impressed. You're a hot piece of ass with a .38, lady."

Coldgrave did not respond, but simply looked out across the lake.

Then the SUV pulled in, and they got up.

With everyone inside, Bradley turned them around and headed for the highway. Coldgrave sat in the navigator's seat to begin the trip home. Fortunately for those in the back, the shotguns had been moved just behind the rear seat. They had not gone far before Bobbie Lee said she did not intend to sit in the middle for the entire four-hour trip. She said that if she couldn't sit somewhere else for at least some of the trip, she was going to take the motorcycle next time.

Lowering her visor, Coldgrave checked her lipstick, then said, "It might be convenient to stop for something to drink. I always get thirstier when traveling."

Bradley winced. "This isn't traveling."

But Gretchin poked him from the back seat. "I'm thirsty, too. Look for a place."

"And when we stop, Ms. Henry," added Coldgrave, "I'll be happy to take your place in the middle." Then she opened her phone and called Willard to tell him that the work had been accomplished, with no one injured, and that they were heading back to the Estate. "But, you have a point, Ms. Henry," she continued, closing the phone. "Independence is indispensable, isn't it? Next time, if you take your motorcycle, I might just take my Jag."

CHAPTER 9

The Estate, November

With a constant look of astonishment on his face, Willard had listened to Gretchin's tirade for nearly five minutes. Keeping the china cup of black tea balanced on his saucer had not been easy, especially when she had broken into profanity.

"It's a goddamn shame," she said, finishing. "If I can't skate this winter, I'm going to be really pissed for Christmas, I can promise you."

He wanted to respond to her, but first winced as George blew noisily across his tea to cool it. He wanted to remind her that she was not a properly trained agent, that she had been merely an advisor initially but then recruited ad hoc and minimally trained, that she was recognized now to be a full agent only insofar as she remained part of this particular team. He wanted to remind her that using such an ad hoc amateur team had been an experiment, and that just because the theory that such a team could at times be more creative and innovative than a traditionally trained team had been shown to be correct, still she should not think of herself as indispensable. He even wanted to tell her that he himself in fact thought her to be more than a little dispensable. But by the grace of God he would hold his tongue.

"I never said you couldn't skate, Ms. Wheeler," he returned, "I simply meant that building a skating pond here might overrun budget. We can figure something out, don't get so upset."

Maggie's entrance with a freshened tea cart provided a break. Gretchin, her brow furrowed under a shock of hair, gave the dragon on her neck a scratch and sat back. Connors and Bobbie Lee crossed their legs in unison and took more tea and cookies. Bradley pretended not to be staring at Gretchin's cleavage. And Packard, serious and grumpy as usual, took another of his wife's fresh chocolate chip cookies and continued to slurp his tea. When Maggie had finished passing out the refreshments, she brought from the kitchen a frosty glass of gin on ice and handed it to Coldgrave.

"Now," said Willard after gulping his tea, "maybe we can get down to serious things."

Gretchin gave him a hard look. "Just what the hell does that mean? Are you saying my skating is trivial? It's my way of relaxing after smearing someone's brains. So, it's not trivial."

"No, no, Ms. Wheeler, really, I'm not saying that at all. But listen, just listen," he stammered. "Let's everyone stop and turn, if you would, to—"

"To what?" she interrupted. "Why don't you just say whatever it is you've come to say, for God's sake? Is that difficult? We're not children, you know."

Then Coldgrave put in, "Gretchin, please, let Bob speak. You have a new project for us, correct, Bob?" Then she tipped the glass and with obvious satisfaction took a substantial drink.

Hesitating, he replied, "Thank you, Mary. Yes, I have a new project for the team, I do. But first, I want to talk a little, if I can, about the last project." Here he put his hands together. "It was well planned and executed, and contingencies were allowed for. It was a little difficult to clean up, but not terribly—three bags, a sanitation unit, and a tow truck, not bad. And thankfully, no cinders this time." Here he shot a disapproving glance in the direction of Connors' icy eyes. "And it met the deadline, no pun intended." He looked around, as if expecting a laugh, but finding only expressions of disinterest, he continued, "I appreciate everything you all did to make it a success. Oh yes, and we all can certainly rejoice that not one of you was hurt."

"*Rejoice*, really?" Gretchin returned, stuffing a wad of hair behind an ear. "What is that? What is *rejoice*? This isn't a church, it's the CIA."

He stared at her helplessly. He had begun to perspire. It was a good thing, he thought, moving his eyes over the pretty face, that he had not gone into the ministry, for with a woman like this in the congregation, he would surely have taken up swearing. "I know that, Ms. Wheeler," he said, "I only meant—"

"And stop calling me that, would you? I'm Gretchin, Bob, Gretchin, okay?"

"All right, sure, okay—*Gretchin*," he replied meekly. "We'll just do first names, fine, only please let me finish, if you would."

She held up both hands, "I'm not stopping you, for God's sake, go ahead."

When Coldgrave held her glass up to catch Maggie's eye, he swallowed heavily, then said, "Well, actually, I just want to say that . . . well, um, why don't we, then, just discuss the next project, would that be all right?" And as no one responded, he continued, "There—are—uh, good grief, I've lost my train of thought."

"Were you going to say," suggested Gretchin, "there are people you want us to fucking kill?"

Swallowing, from sheer frustration, "I wasn't going to put it that way, of course, but yes, we do have a new project for the team, as I've said, one that involves the—*removal*—of a certain individual who has been determined by the Agency to pose a present danger to the interests of the United States. He is, the individual, not presently in this country."

"Good," she came back, clinking her cup and saucer, "because we're not actually, legally, supposed to be operating inside the U.S., are we?"

Clearly annoyed, Coldgrave put in, "Gretchin, I think I went over that before. Please don't ask Bob to address that, if you will. Besides, are you concerned about the law?"

Cocking her head, "No, I'm not, I just wanted to see what he would say."

Straightening his back, as if to regain his composure, he gave George a look of incredulity, then said to them, "This individual is somewhat of a hothead, I'll tell you that right off. He owns multiple handguns, and so, being emotionally volatile, is to be considered quite dangerous. But he's not a thug. He's actually a computer guy, which is how he conducts the business. The business is coordinating, as a kind of kingpin, the murder of officials in developing countries. The whole situation's a mess frankly and has to be cleaned up ASAP. The problem is his where-abouts—he's off the screen at present. But we have a reliable tip that he will be entering the United States to go to, of all things, a computer show. Anyway, I wanted to let you be thinking about it, but we won't move until the middle of April. The show is to be held at an expo center near Atlanta. I'll send you a packet with photos and more info in a week or so. So, how does that sound, inter-esting?"

Bradley cleared his throat. "I think it sounds very interesting, Bob. Who's going?"

Momentarily, "Feeling left out?"

"I don't want to just drive the car."

"No, of course not, I understand, and there's no reason someone else can't drive, if they're not needed elsewhere. But let's be realistic, you're perfect as a driver. You know machines extremely well and can drive well, and you can also do the—"

"The killing?"

A groan. "Well, that's crude, but yes, you're good with a gun also, let's say. So, don't feel bad, you've done your share of the, uh, work, and you'll no doubt get to do more, so to speak. But on this one, I think, we'll keep it simple and only send in Kelly and Bobbie Lee again, unless the situation changes at go time. Thanks, Bradley, though, you're doing a great job, all of you are. . . . Are there any other questions?" His eyes then went to Connors, he did not know why, perhaps instinctively, as if predicting somehow that she would speak. But when she did, it nearly startled him.

Connors crossed her legs. "What're we supposed to do untel than?"

Another one that he would have been lucky enough to get in the congregation, he thought. Look at that beautiful face, the blond hair. He imagined her body, scarred from bullet holes. It must be wonderful to watch her in action, reaching up under the shirt for the gun, ripping it down, and sending hell fire at someone, turning his face into hamburger. Shuddering inside, he answered, "Good question, Kelly. Just take a vacation if you can, lots of them, whatever you want." He looked into the unflinching, defiant eyes, which looked back at him, as though seeing through him.

CHAPTER 10

As the winter moved in, the Lancaster County farm country became sugar-coated, then snow-laden. The trees surrounding the Estate grew heavy with ice and snow and made everyone think of Osipov and his tales of Moscow and the KGB. When his Christmas card arrived from Russia, they talked of him and recalled his charm and dependable character. But such reminiscing was avoided, for it inevitably conjured images of Martina and her recounting of her family's escape from East Germany.

Throughout the snow season Bradley manned the Estate's tractor plow, keeping the driveway to the highway cleared and salted. He did not mind so much, since he himself needed access to the highway for visiting the nearby towns and cities. He had volunteered for the duty to help fill Osipov's vacancy. Besides, if he could demonstrate his strength or prowess through executing menial chores, so much the better. Occasionally he would suggest to Gretchin that he had cleared the snow so the two of them could drive to Philly and take in dinner and a movie. Rarely did she turn him down.

For her, winter was boring as hell and the choice was obvious, either find something of interest to do or sit around and eat too much or drink too much. The skating had not worked out; Willard's message was that since no funds were available to install even a modest skating slab, she might get herself to a professional rink. That left reading, which she did enjoy, and television, which she did not. So, taking Bradley up on an excursion to the city meant sheer survival. If he put his hands on her during the movie, she might let him or not, but she wasn't about to just sit around the farm, as she would say, to decline like some goddamn housewife.

For three weeks during February, when the Packards were in Florida, Gretchin and Bobbie Lee took over in the kitchen and with managing the household. Packard himself had not required a vacation, but would have been content, as he put it, to spend the winter months practicing at the range or cleaning and repairing weapons in his room. Maggie, on the other hand, who found cold weather loathsome, had insisted that he either go with her to Miami or the Bahamas. He chose the former.

Upon the Packards' return, Bobbie Lee and Connors bundled up and left for a month-long motorcycle trip to the Jersey shore. Throughout March they wandered cold beaches and roamed lonesome boardwalks. In the evenings, they would rumble up to a restaurant, stride in with their helmets, and try new seafood dishes, and each night they would stay at a different inn or bed and breakfast. While in Cape May they took fried-shrimp platters onto the docks for lunch at the Lobster House and spent a quiet hour at the Lucky Bones Restaurant for dinner. During their last day, they visited the approximate place at Cape May Point where they had shot the two targets and their bodyguards as they picnicked on the beach. And on the return trip to Lancaster County, they pulled into the Farley Service Plaza along the Atlantic City Expressway for coffee and donuts.

For her own part, Coldgrave often left to spend a few days in New York. There she would visit with family and go shopping with old friends. At parties she would refer to Pennsylvania by calling it her Siberia and declaring that she had been sent there by the Czar. But it was there, and sometimes seemingly only there, among the wealthy elite she had grown up with, that she was able to freshen up, as she put it, with a martini or two and regain her true equilibrium. Returning, she would park in the bleak old stable, trudge across the icy walkway, and ask if Bradley wouldn't be good enough to bring in her luggage from the Jag.

But of course everyone knew that with the arrival of spring, or at least April, whether spring came with it or not, all attention would have to be centered on readying for the new project. Toward the end of March, Willard called with fresh info on the target and to say he had definitely decided to send only Bobbie Lee and Connors. They could fly down or even drive, it didn't matter.

"I wonder," said Connors at breakfast, "ef they'll ever start havin' us use explosives."

"I wouldn't think so, girl," replied Bobbie Lee, stabbing a pancake. "You'll jist have to wait for that until you git back to Irelan'."

"Oh, actually, I prefaer joost usin' a gun."

Bradley, wincing at the thought of using explosives, said, "Poison I can see, but a bomb, no way."

When Coldgrave, who had come in from New York the previous evening, sat down in a T-shirt, jeans and high-heels, the others stopped eating till she had scooted her chair in.

"That's nice," Bradley said, "I didn't know you wore T-shirts or jeans."

"I do on occasion," she returned pleasantly, her right eye falling upon him briefly.

"Wonder how much they cost. Oh, that's right, you wouldn't know."

"Bradley," said Gretchin, holding her coffee up, "don't be an ass."

He grinned mischievously. "Just asking."

"You're a liar, and now you're not just an ass, you're an asshole."

"I was just asking, Gretchin. Can't I ask?"

"No."

"Okay," he said, "I won't ask. Forget it."

"I will, stooge."

Coldgrave smiled. "Gretchin may forget it, Bradley, but I will not." And reaching for the pot of coffee and filling her cup, she added, "You didn't look at me the way you usually look at women when they're taking their seat, did you?"

"Oh, yeah?" he returned, meeting her gaze. "What's that supposed to mean?" Then he looked around at the others. Maggie's eyes were fixed upon him, her usual smile absent. Gretchin's eyes were aflame, as though ready to explode. Packard's were upon the coffee in his cup. Bobbie Lee's were filled with the entertainment of someone watching a trapped criminal. Connors' were glazed with indifference. Finally he looked back at Coldgrave and said, "You noticed that?"

"I did," she replied, taking a sip of the coffee, leaving a red lipstick mark on the cup.

"Well," he said, "maybe I didn't find you interesting. Do I have to find you interesting?"

"Certainly not, Bradley. You have a right to be interested in whomever you wish and for whatever reason."

"Then what's the problem?"

"I don't have a problem with you, Bradley. Do you have one with me?"

He swallowed. "Yeah, maybe I do."

"How so?" she queried, taking another sip and leaving another mark.

He looked at the lips, then answered, "Maybe I like to know who I'm talking to, a man or a woman. Which are you?"

She smiled. "Perhaps I'm neither, or both, or something in between, or perhaps I don't know, myself."

The palpable silence in the room was broken only when he cleared his throat. With a faint frown, he said, "That's confusing for me."

"Yes, well, I'm sorry, Bradley. Reality is often such, though, isn't it? Only fantasy seems clear."

Another frown. "So, you don't know how you see yourself?"

She lifted the cup, then put it back down. "At this point I see myself as a woman. Is that acceptable?"

He wanted to say *not with your equipment*, but held his peace.

Letting it go, she said, "Well, everybody, I have some news. I spoke with Bob last night, and he now wants Bradley, Gretchin and me to go to Atlanta."

Bobbie Lee made a click with her tongue. "Why'd he scrap us?"

"He didn't. He said he wants to see how the three of us work together. Anyway, we are to fly down and then use a rental car for the project. We won't be staying, it's a one-day thing. We'll go directly, or at least semi-directly, to the exposition center, execute the project, and then fly home."

Yeah, thought Bradley, the *semi-directly* will mean a bar stop for you, won't it, sweetheart? Instead he said, "An expo center, in broad daylight?"

"That's correct."

"And one day? How does that make sense?"

"Bradley," put in Gretchin, "don't ask that, please."

Ignoring this, he said, "But where's the margin for error? I mean, stuff goes wrong."

"There's not a lot," replied Coldgrave, "almost none. The show is from ten to four, but he could leave an hour into it, who knows? The center has only two public men's rooms, meaning they'll be crowded, and one inside lunch area. The parking lot is fairly large, but that means end of the show and even less margin. His booking is for an inn not far from the expo center, so if pressed, we might actually have to hit him in his room. Of course, he will probably get something to eat after the show. We can think about contingencies, but my guess is that we'll simply have to locate him, wait a reasonable amount of time to isolate him, then hit him and try to get out as neatly as possible. If things go wrong, they go wrong."

"Oh boy," said Gretchin, "this sounds really cute. Thanks a lot, Bob."

"The only leeway for the project itself," Coldgrave continued, "is that since the target has now booked his flight, intel now knows where he'll be coming from. Bob says that if we miss the target, an agent will be on his return flight and can perhaps do something once there. ... But if we miss and the target doesn't take his return flight, but instead disappears, intending to establish himself here somewhere, well, he might never be stopped."

Then Maggie stood up. "Ah, that's the timer. Would anybody like blueberry cobbler?"

CHAPTER 11

Atlanta, Georgia, April 2014

The parking lot was dark and already wet from light rain as Bradley wheeled the Toyota around, then backed into a space. Beside him, Gretchin had been fidgeting since leaving the airport. Behind him, Coldgrave lowered her window and looked out at the sky.

"You know what's going to happen, right?" said Gretchin, checking herself in the visor mirror. "We'll get him and it'll rain like hell—it's going to rain, it says—and they'll cancel our flight back. Three assassins stuck in an international airport after a job. Fucking super, that's what I say."

His eyes looking for entering cars, "Come on, don't be negative, we'll work with it. Help me look, now, we have to find this guy. You're good at this, you watch TV."

"I can't stand TV. Who watches TV, bub? You put more time in than I ever could, you and your sports. Besides, what's TV got to do with it?"

"You recognize all the stars, *and* their wives and girlfriends, *and* their ridiculous children. So, help me look for this guy, would you? Stop looking in the mirror."

She flipped the visor up as Coldgrave said, "But she's right, it's supposed to be a heavy rain. Actually, it may help us."

Gretchin looked back at her. "How? It'll just make it harder to spot him."

"I don't like the rain. It means mud, and mud is distasteful. But, you can move about, even hide, in a mess. Look at that sky."

After an hour, Bradley said, "We've got to get in there. We've missed him out here. And who wouldn't? Boy, what a rain—cats and puppies."

Through the dark heavy rain they made their way under three umbrellas to the entrance. Paying their fee, Bradley took his umbrella back from Gretchin, who had not bothered to shake it out for him, and with annoyance simply pulled it tight and velcroed it. Once inside the exhibition hall, they spread out. Despite the weather, the show seemed well attended.

It was half an hour before Coldgrave's phone vibrated. Opening it, she read, *Found him. Toshiba near the back.* Within minutes she reached the vendor's booth.

"I've been following him," said Gretchin. "That's him over there in the blue polo."

"I see him," said Coldgrave.

Then Bradley stood beside them. About thirty feet away, the target, embroiled in a conversation with the company rep, seemed so engaged that

Bradley said, "One in the spine and one in the head, right? Is that lucky?"

"No, try stupid," remarked Gretchin. "Maybe you want to shoot him in front of everybody, but I don't. Let's just follow him, wait for something better. Mary?"

"Surely," said Coldgrave. "And spread out. Bradley, we'll stick to him, you follow farther back."

Just as they were separating, the man turned, scanned the area, then turned back to the rep. When a laptop was put before him, he bent forward to watch the images as the rep did the scrolling. Then he said something to the rep, stepped beside the booth, and walked toward the curtain.

But they were on him, and soon Coldgrave texted Bradley, *He is in restroom. Not following.* When he arrived, they spread out again and watched the doorway.

After a few minutes, Bradley walked over to Coldgrave. "Maybe ten guys have gone in there, and they've all come out."

"I know," she said. "All right, take a look."

Thirty seconds later he returned. "He's not there. There's an exit that opens out onto the parking lot. I think we've lost him." He watched her face fill with anxiety, so that she seemed grotesque. Then Gretchin was there, and he felt somehow responsible for losing the man.

"Bradley," said Coldgrave, "go back in and follow the exit out to the lot, then sweep around toward our car. We'll meet you there. Keep your eyes open. Go."

As the two women left the show through the main entrance the rain began to fall furiously, graying the car-filled parking lot. Coldgrave motioned for Gretchin to go left, while she went right. Nearly with rage the rain now beat upon their umbrellas. She watched till Gretchin had disappeared. Then quickly, watchfully she began to move up and down the rows and between cars. A text came through from Bradley, *Did not find. Going to car.*

Already in their row, she made her way toward the Toyota. Then she saw the wet blue polo as the man stepped beside the Toyota and stood at the driver's window. Steadily, with the rain beating upon his head, streaming down his face, he motioned with a gun for the window to be lowered. He was speaking, but she could not hear him for the pounding of the rain.

"Put it down," he commanded, raising his voice and grinning menacingly. "Put the fucking window down, guy!" As the glass came down he shoved the gun in through the window. "Great, now I can see your rat's face. On my ass, huh? I wonder why. I guess we both know, don't we? Know somethin' else? I'm gonna blow your nose right off your face . . . Get ready to die, fucker."

But it was then that Coldgrave stepped from behind the adjacent car, brought her .38 up, and fired—*Blat!* The shot hit the man in the temple, simultaneously knocking his head to the side and dropping him flat out on the pavement. Taking two quick steps, she fired again, down into his head, *Pop! Pop! Pop!* And with Bradley's ghastly face staring at her from the open window, she said to him, "Once more, just for fun." Then she leaned over, put the muzzle down to just beside the man's nose, fired, and blew it off. "Gracious," she exclaimed, "wonder where that ricochet went!"

Bradley had jumped as the gun went off, but now sat immoveable. He watched as she stood up and turned to look at him again, the gun smoking in her gloved hand, the pouring rain streaming through her hair. Oddly now, even with that left eye looking out to the side, she no longer seem grotesque. He looked into her right eye and then followed the red lips, for she was speaking.

"So, be a gentleman," she said cheerily, raising her voice to be heard over the pounding rain, "I think I've lost my umbrella."

The Estate, Early May

"The winter's just about done around here," offered Willard, accepting the cup and saucer from Maggie. "We saw flowers coming up the drive. The place looks great." And getting a nod from George, he added, "I should do more gardening. I enjoy growing things, and flowers really can strut their stuff in the spring, can't they?"

"Oh yes," agreed Maggie, holding a plate of cookies before him. "I've been waiting all winter."

"But I thought you went to Florida for, what, a month?"

"No, three weeks, Bob, but trust me, it seemed like three days."

They had been waiting for the others to come in, but now they began to arrive and take their seats. He watched cautiously as Gretchin moved past him, poured herself a cup of tea, then sat to look at him, a smug expression on her face. Then Connors, as if barely willing to acknowledge his presence, and Bobbie Lee, flexing her muscles, first the forearms, then the triceps, like some circus performer. His gaze moved to the rubber butts of Packard's magnums as they rode in their rig. What a group. With each encounter, he became more convinced of their strangeness. When they were all seated, he put cup and saucer together and spoke.

"All right," he said cheerily, "so, that was a good one, don't you think? Efficient, yes? Just down and back, right? How about it, Mary, what's your assessment?"

But Maggie, who seemed intentionally to interrupt him, asked Coldgrave what she would like to drink. Waiting silent until the frosty glass of beer was brought from the kitchen, he marveled at the woman's sheer capacity for alcohol. Determined not to speak until he had been answered properly, he sipped his tea.

"I think," replied Coldgrave at last, "yes, the project went well. Efficiently? I suppose so. Let's just say, it was fun."

In his chair, Tai Ping yawned, putting his eyes briefly upon Willard.

"Look," said Willard, "I only stopped in to say hi and to let you all know that the next project won't be until August, if then. It might be given to another team, so I don't want to get your hopes up. Until then, just relax. Gretchin, you'll be getting some swimming in, I suppose?" When her blank expression told him she had no intention of answering, he cleared his throat and took up his cup. "Bradley, the report said you had somewhat of a close call. But, you don't look any the worse, as they say."

Bradley's eyes went first to Coldgrave, then to Willard. "Yeah," he replied, "I guess I did. No big deal, though. I wasn't paying attention, and it was raining, and everything was crazy. But thanks to Mary here, I'm fine, ready to go."

Gretchin, who had been waiting for him to say something stupid, so she could pounce, merely said, "We all got a little wet, but had a good time. It was fun."

Bradley's eyes went to Coldgrave. Taking in the pink top, the cool pants, he said, smiling, "Hey, Mary, those are great shoes. I'll bet they were expensive."

Returning the smile, she replied, "I wouldn't know, actually."

CHAPTER 12

Willard gave his leather chair a single spin, then sat down. Removing the lid from his coffee and then setting the cup aside, he opened the file and began reading through the biography. *Gretchin Wheeler, born 1955 of Swedish parents. Musician, artist, photographer. Former art teacher at middle school, along with colleagues Martina Jung [Osipov] and Margaret Swift-Jones [Packard], with Bradley Hopkins as principal. Uncle killed by Russians in Finnish Winter War. . . . Creative, volatile, keenly disrespectful, profane.* He stopped, took a few sips of the coffee, then continued.

It was not until lunchtime that he finished the files for all the team, including that for Coldgrave. He sat back, his head sinking into the soft leather. He looked toward the ceiling. And just who was this Mary Coldgrave he thought he knew so well? Why had she been demoted? Oh, certainly the record didn't read that way, as in fact he had just read it, but he knew it should have. The sloppy stuff she had overseen in the Florida project could not have resulted in anything other than demotion. She may have accepted the idea that being moved down to a team leadership position was a mere opportunity for further education, but he had not. He was not going to be delusional, but realistic, and in fact, it was an unmistakable demotion. But why then had he been chosen to take her place as team contact? What was the team's greatest deficiency, and how could he help? What would make them a more professional, efficient team? He personally had never bought into Kessler's theory that amateurs could be more creative than professionals, or that a certain social dysfunctionality among team members could be an asset. If others had accepted the team's successes as proof the theory was correct, he had not, for he had found that evidence to be fuzzy and its interpretation problematic.

He looked at the clock. He would go to lunch and give the whole thing a good think-through. If he was going to be realistic about identifying problems, he should be realistic about correcting them. It would be silly, for instance, to attempt to correct Gretchin's vagrant mouth by taping it shut. But discipline never hurt anybody, either. In fact, it was the core truth behind a professional character. Yes, the team needed him, the Agency needed him, which was why, realistically, he had been brought to the position.

The Estate, June

"We're so glad, Bob, you've come to visit," said Maggie, holding forth a carefully tailored sample of her lemonade. "Now, just enjoy yourself and let me know if you need anything."

"I will," he replied. "Thanks, Maggie. Ah, this looks wonderful, hits the spot. I love lemonade." And placing the glass on the table, he followed her swaying skirt as she returned to the kitchen. But he was not a fool, and the report had been clear that, although appearing to be quite domestic, she could unlease the contents of her five-shot revolver before you could count to three. Ah, but this was the life. The house, the pool, the lemonade—the imagery was convincing, accentuated by the slightest of breezes as it passed under the umbrella to cool him.

He only checked himself when Gretchin emerged from the house and, towel under her arm, flip-flopped her way in his direction. She swayed as she walked, the way a stripper might, her yellow swimsuit moving with her, as if it was a cat's skin. And the red hair, the sunglasses, the tattooed neck. Lord, what a temptress.

"Hi, Bob," she cooed, spreading the towel over a chair at the next table, "how's the water?"

He swallowed. "Not bad, I think, but I only put a toe in." It was only then that he noticed she had deliberately chosen not to sit with him. "Do the Packards swim?"

"Some," she replied, curling her toes and running a hand down her stomach. "I do a lot, and Kelly and Bobbie Lee swim in the evenings. I think we all enjoy having a pool."

"Well," he said, "it's good the cost is justified, then."

She did not look at him as she said, "If you're looking for justification, you could probably replace all the water in this pool with the blood we've shed in the Agency's service."

He wanted to respond, but instead turned to watch as Coldgrave emerged from the house and walked toward them. He had not seen her in a swimsuit before and now made a mental note that her walk seemed even more sensuous, even sensual. His eyes went first to the sunglasses, then for some reason fell to the elaborate bathing shoes, then rose very slowly, as she got closer, until they had taken in the rest of her. Involuntarily he swallowed hard.

"So, do you like it?" she said to him, spreading her towel over a chair next to Gretchin's.

Momentarily, "What? Uh, I do, Mary, very much. It's quite idyllic, yes."

A pleasant smile. "The pleasure is ours, I'm sure."

Then he stood and said, "I might try the water, would you mind?"

"Not at all," said Gretchin, moving her sun-glasses up, "help yourself. Drink it, if you like."

He looked at her, but only briefly, her gorgeous skin aglow, her smile like that of a tiger about to kill the world; then at Coldgrave, her left eye looking outward, her own smile like that of a woman about to make love to the world. He turned, as if away from them, put his goggles up and dove into the sparkling aqua water. For a few moments he moved under the surface, swimming through the shafts of sunlight. Coming up, he saw that Bradley, who gave him a wave, was making his way around the pool.

Falling into the chair next to Willard's, Bradley put his feet up and then set his lemonade on the concrete. "You ladies look nice," he said. "Want me to get you some drinks, maybe a gin on the rocks and a lemonade?" Then he left them and in a few minutes returned with the drinks.

"You're helpful," said Gretchin. "None for yourself?"

He said he'd already had some lemonade, and she said he'd make a great lifeguard and offered to get him some zinc oxide for his nose. Then Willard climbed from the water and dried himself with his towel.

"This is the life," Bradley said. "Right, Bob?"

Willard spread the towel and took a seat. "It sure is. But as Gretchin points out, you guys have done a lot in the Agency's service, your country's service."

A chuckle. "She said that?"

"I only said Agency, not country," said Gretchin.

"Oh," returned Willard jovially, "an unnecessary correction, I think."

But she came back with, "Is it, Bob? Is it unnecessary?"

Lord, he thought, here it comes. "Well, in a way, yes. To serve the Agency is to serve your country, obviously. So, Gretchin, you're a patriot, whether you admit it or not."

"Really? Actually, I misspoke, I'm not even serving the Agency, let alone the country."

He cleared his throat and nearly whined, "Then why do you do it? And I think that's a fair question."

"I'm not sure. Maybe because I feel like it right now. Tomorrow, who knows?"

"So," he said, "you're not a patriot?"

"Hell no."

He met her aqua eyes, then said, "Do you think the Agency should be happy about that?"

She lifted her glass, took a drink, then replied, "I don't give a shit if they're happy with it or not. If they don't like it, they can fire me."

"What's your point in saying all this?"

"Maybe I'm just being contrary," she retorted. "Maybe I'm resisting control."

"But control is the essence of discipline, wouldn't you say?"

"Sure," she replied, "I'd agree with that."

Bradley, who had had enough, put in, "Come on, why so serious, everybody? It's a beautiful day. Gorgeous women, good-looking guys, and we spend the time arguing?"

The change in the conversation was enforced with the appearance of Connors and Bobbie Lee, who with towels and drinks, began to make their way around the pool. They were close, chatting as they walked. No one spoke as they approached, but Bradley dropped his gaze, for both were in two-piece suits. Bobbie Lee's suit, clearly the more modest, seemed to accentuate the rocky muscles of her hard body. Connors', a borderline-risqué affair, exposed not simply her well-formed body, but seemed to showcase its numerous scars from bullet holes.

"How old are you, Bob?" queried Bradley as the women pulled chairs from one of the tables.

"What? Oh, uh, thirty-seven, this year."

"Same age as Mary, then."

Willard's eyes found Connors and Bobbie Lee again, then Coldgrave. "Yes, same as Mary. Why do you ask?"

Bradley shook his head. "Not sure. But it's good to be alive, isn't it?"

"Certainly, Bradley, yes it is."

CHAPTER 13

It was during dinner that evening that Willard put out the question as to everyone's religious affiliation. When Maggie warned that such conversation might serve only to cool her fresh apple pie, he assured her he had no intention of stirring things up.

"How about you, then, Maggie?" he queried amicably. "Do you go to church anywhere? Oh, and this roast is wonderful, just delicious, thanks so much. And the mashed potatoes, are they grown around here?"

"I have no idea, but I get everything from a local market, and it always seems fresh." Then she smiled. "No, I don't go to church. I went to the Church of England as a child, but I don't go anywhere now."

"Why not, may I ask?"

Pleasantly, "I see the organized church as kind of a business, you know. It's cute, but not quite real. Am I saying that right?"

Hesitantly, "Okay. . . . And so, how about your husband here?"

Packard, the butts of his magnums almost touching the tablecloth, looked at him suspiciously. "Well, God? Sure, why not? But, affiliation with a group of some kind? I don't think so, pal."

"Same here," piped Gretchin. "God's great, as they say, beer's good, and people are pretty much fucking nuts."

His eyes went closed for a moment. "Thank you, Gretchin, for that profane insight."

"What did you want me to say?" she retorted. "And why is it your business what I believe or where or if I go to church? Those things are usually considered personal and private."

Chuckling, he shrugged. "This *is* the CIA—is anything personal or private? They know what my basic beliefs are and where I go to church."

"They have that information about me too, about all of us. Why don't you go back and read the files again? And you can consider that an interrogative question. Seriously, I would like to know the answer. You're being methodical, you're going around the table, everyone can see that, and I'd like to know why the hell you're doing it."

He held up his hands. "I'm just asking, Gretchin, that's all. Information in files can be misleading, everyone knows that. I wanted to know just for myself. Don't take offense, really."

"Bullshit," she returned, pointing at him. "You never *just* ask anything, you always calculate, it's in your DNA. You're after something, and you're not saying what it is. I think you're going to insert your nose so far as to suggest we actually go to church or synagogue or something, aren't you?"

"No, no, don't take it that way," he said, frustration in his tone. "I'm just asking, Gretchin. It interests me."

Tired of the circularity of this exchange, Bobbie Lee said, "Well, Killy here's a Catholic and swears by the Holy Virgin, but I'm nothin' religiously. I believe in God and Jesus and all that, but I need a religious support group like I need a flatter chest."

"Your chast," put in Connors, after slurping her tea, "ain't flat, no fuckin' way."

Again his eyes went closed. How had he gotten himself into this? "Okay, okay," he muttered, "well, I'm seeing more where everybody's coming from. Okay, sure. ... Um, Mr. Hopkins here, buddy, any thoughts? I mean, do you go to church?"

Bradley pressed his back against his chair and wiped his nose with his thumb. "I used to be a Baptist. It's kind of American, I think, being a Baptist, I mean, well, I mean, sort of. But I don't go anymore or anything. Maybe I don't belong there."

Willard looked at him earnestly. "You should go again, you might like it."

"What would I say about my job?"

"Well—you could just say that you—" came the answer, "or no, better, you could go for trans-parency, which is very *in*, and just tell them you work for the CIA and let it go, what would be wrong with that? You might really like it. You and Gretchin could both go, you'd have a great time. They have activities and things."

"Oh, I don't know," said Bradley. "Maybe sometime."

Willard picked up his cup, then put it back down. "Mary, how about you? I never knew much about you, even in the office. Do you go to church?"

She looked at him. "But as the team's contact, you've read my file, too, correct?"

He reddened, then stammered, his head bobbing, "I—well, yes, I have looked at it. Sort of."

"You've perused it, correct?"

The redness seemed to increase. "Yes, I guess I have, Mary, but I'd still like to hear what you might have to say about it. Files can be wrong, very wrong sometimes. So, what is your religious affiliation?"

"None, Bob. I'm a Christian. Yes, I believe in God. No, I don't believe in people. No, I don't go to church."

Nearly against his will, his eyes softened. He had never been able to resist her charm. For the life of him, he could not explain it, other than to blame it on some biological magnetism. Date her? No, he no longer wished to date her. But when she spoke, on virtually any subject, or simply walked into the room, there was something about her, something in her manner, her person, that he could not resist. So, now he looked at her and said nothing.

Connors stuck her fork into her meat. "And how 'bout the inquisitor here? What do you believe?"

Forcing from his mind images of her bikini and scarred-over bullet holes, he replied, "I—well, I believe in God certainly, and I go to church. I'm a Presbyterian."

"Aw," Bobbie Lee moaned, "they're stiff, too stiff for me, that's for sure. Bet you wear a suit there, don't you?"

"Yes, as a matter of fact, I do. But they're not as formal as you might think."

"Well," she returned, "I think they're crazy, and some of 'em are worse'n Pentecostals, which is at the opposite end of the spectrum, I understand that, but still, I think they're nuts, with all that Reformed stuff goin' on and pickin' people out of the hat to go to hell. Jeez, no thank you."

He looked at her, then took a sip of his coffee.

After dinner, Maggie and Gretchin cleared the table and put away the leftovers and pie, while Willard shot pool with Bradley and Packard. Then Packard turned the TV on, and they all watched a few innings of baseball.

Willard stayed the night, sleeping in the guest room. In the morning, following breakfast and two cups of Maggie's specially brewed coffee, as he called it, he gave them all a wave, got into the gray sedan, and drove back to New York.

"The poor man," lamented Maggie as she watched his car disappear, "he's so confused."

Coldgrave nodded. "Yes, quite. But then, who isn't?"

"Don't get existential on me, I've got dishes to do, and I'm convinced it's important and that I'll have to answer to everybody, at least to Lenny, if I burn the dinner tonight."

If it had been difficult for Willard to visit with them, not just as a team but individually, with all their pathetic eccentricities, surely it had also reassured him of their need for greater discipline.

But what was he to do? He was not, after all, either their drill instructor or their pastor. And oh, that Gretchin, what a mouth. And Connors, talk about insane. Again he had to force the images of her from his mind. But as the miles clicked off, the images he did not force from his mind were those of Mary Coldgrave.

The mirror at her dresser seemed dark as Maggie looked into it, dark enough for her to see Martina's face instead of her own. But life was like that, it caught you at a bad moment, cornered you, and made you see faces of loved ones it had itself deliberately taken from you. It seemed actually to wait until you were hopeful that you had dealt with the loss and had made reasonable attempts to forget, then came out of the shadows and attacked you. It needed no tools of its own, for such were readily available in the images of your mind and the memories of your heart. If life could be beautiful and healing, it could also be ugly and destructive. It kissed you, then waited for you, around the corner and in the shadows, and when it jumped you, it tried its best to kill you.

Then she watched as he entered and stood behind her. In that same dark mirror she looked at him, the grizzly killer who had come to love her. She did not turn around as he spoke.

"Want to watch a movie tonight?" And when she did not answer, "Or we could take the car and go out somewhere."

"Where would we go?"

"I don't know," he rasped, "to a bar, or a movie. Just to get out. Would you want to do that?"

"You're looking through me again, aren't you?"

"Well, you seem pretty sad. You're thinking of her."

"She would have been seventy-five this August, still very healthy, very beautiful."

He put his hands on her shoulders. They were gnarled hands, stained with gun oil and from cartridge flash, hands that should not be used to comfort such a tender woman bearing such a burden of grief. But they were the only hands he had, and he used them.

"I'm so sorry," he said. "You two were really close, I know, and it's silly to try to make you feel better. But I love you, and I want to help. I can't do anything, I know. I'm so sorry, sweetie. She was such a wonderful person. I don't think Osipov will ever get over it, either."

"No, I think not."

Their eyes met briefly in the mirror, and when she looked back at her face, he said, "Why don't we just stay in tonight? I've got some maintenance to do on Bobbie Lee's P-64, so I'll leave you alone, and I'll see you later, okay?"

Then he left, and she sat looking into the mirror for a long time.

CHAPTER 14

During July, as the weather turned hot and humid, the pool became the utility of choice for cooling off. Almost daily everyone spent at least some time at the pool. They would swim, lounge under the umbrellas, and talk for long hours. Often they ate lunch there. Maggie would roll the tea cart out with freshly steeped tea, saying that sometimes hot drinks cooled you more than cold ones. Poolside became the favorite place to read, to discuss, or even to watch a ball game on TV. If Bradley and Gretchin were in the pool, Packard might bring a few guns out and clean them. If Maggie joined him, he would put down the guns to talk and enjoy what he said was the sweet life. Coldgrave usually read novels or talked about life among the rich, sharing tidbits of high society and their opulent parties. Connors and Bobbie Lee, practically inseparable, would pass hours at a time looking at magazines, drinking, and talking about life in Ireland and Tennessee.

It was on such a sultry day that Coldgrave's new Bentley Continental was delivered and the Jaguar taken away. Bradley, who had been hosing down the Corvette, turned the water off and strode over to look.

"White," he remarked, "jeez, who would want a white car?"

But she knew he was teasing, and said, "Well, it's a Mediterranean color. One might see it at the Casino de Monte-Carlo, for instance."

"What's the horsepower on something like this?"

"Over six hundred, I was told."

He gave a low whistle. "Good gracious. And where are the attendants? You'll probably need special water brought in just to wash it."

"I wouldn't know about that, actually. I don't know about washing things."

His eyes moved slowly over the gleaming car, as though it was a beautiful woman. "How much?"

"I wouldn't know that either, I'm afraid. Sorry."

Looking through a window at the interior, he gave his head a shake. "Where do you get something like this fixed?"

"My mechanics in New York should be okay with it. They took care of my Jag. But it shouldn't need much, it's a Bentley, you know."

"Yeah, I know, I know. I've never seen one in person before, but I know. Guess I wouldn't want to eat a burger and fries in it. . . . What about the truck trash on the road, the sand and dust? This finish is unbelievable."

"Oh," she replied, pulling her sunglasses off, "I don't worry about things like that. It'll be fine, I'm sure."

"Well, lady," he said, straightening his back, "I'm impressed. I guess they'll be kissing your ass wherever you drive this thing."

Then he felt bad that he had said it that way, and wished he could take it back. But as she seemed to ignore the comment, he went back to hosing down the Corvette.

Toward the end of July Willard came again for a visit, this time, on business. He sat by the pool with George, photos spread across a table, with cups of Maggie's tea and apple pie.

"You realize," he said, his eyes on Connors as she climbed from the pool, "that you folks are standing at the gate, as they say. You are protectors of the palace of the western world, if that's not being too grandiose." And with a sweep of his hand, "Which is why the Agency has invested in all this."

"Yeah," said Gretchin, "killers don't come cheap." And when he frowned at this, she said, "And obviously you think the palace is worth protecting."

"Of course it is, you know it is, Gretchin. You put your life on the line, precisely because you know it is."

"You're sure that's why I do it, huh?"

"I have confidence it is, yes. You believe the country's worth protecting, don't you?"

"Hell no," she returned emphatically. And after taking a sip from her beer, "What makes the country worth protecting is me."

He picked up one of the photos and with a groan said, "All right, I think we might skip the philosophy and start cutting mustard here."

But Bobbie Lee put in, "Bradley's the only one here that marches in step, I guess you know. He's the patriot, the rist of us are jis' loose canons."

He hated to hear people talk like this. Why was life like that? Why did it give you a congregation that insisted on going out to a bar after your sermon? You dedicated yourself, you prepared, worked all week, in fact. You even delivered the message with conviction and attempted to throw in a little pizzazz to keep them interested. Then you stood there and shook their hands. But yeah, they showed you their backsides and walked straight to the bar. Unable to hide his distress, he sighed grievously, looked down, then simply continued.

"The project I have for you," he said, "involves the capture of two computers, both laptops."

"*Capture*?" said Gretchin, "that's a little melo-dramatic, isn't it?"

Not looking at her, but blinking nervously from sheer distress, he again continued, "It's vital that we get the information on them, but the pro-gramming interests us, too. They're gaming computers, very powerful. The two men who use them, both geek types, coders and all that, are deemed by the Agency to be criminals of the first order. They've written and executed a program that hacks and destroys military computers for medical facilities. Five facilities have been hit, affecting heart monitors in critical care units. So far, ten veterans have died as a result. And this is where it gets weird, their next target will be an unspecified major pediatric hospital somewhere outside the U.S. So, the Agency wants the guys put down and the computers retrieved intact."

"So, as usual," said Coldgrave, "they must not be allowed to enter prison, correct?"

"Quite."

"And where are these characters?"

He did not answer immediately, but instead found himself staring at Packard, who was clearly not paying the slightest attention. The gray man, in T-shirt and shorts, simply slouched before his glass of dark beer. One of his big Smiths protruded from his waistband, as if about to fall out. His other gun, obviously loaded, he had laid on the glass tabletop. Willard looked down at the heavy barrel, for it had been left pointing directly at himself and George.

"You know," said Packard, waving a hand at Bradley, as if Willard had not even been talking, "That Bentley's quite a car, it'll probably run on vodka."

"Uh, Mr. Packard," said Willard, "I just want to continue about the project, if I may. That okay?"

"Sure," was the grim reply. "What the hell do I care?"

Willard cleared his throat. "Well, that's the thing, Mary, the targets are virtually completely mobile. Right now, they're in England. They've booked a flight to Philadelphia for mid-August. Everywhere they go, they rent a van or an SUV, and simply stay mobile, using open Wi-Fi networks. They're terribly elusive."

"So," she returned, "we may have to actually chase them."

"Correct," he replied, his eyes going to the still-disinterested Packard. "You folks seem to be pretty good at that kind of thing."

Bobbie Lee flexed her forearms, and looked at Connors. "Guess we'll have to git the Harley tuned up, then. Looks like we might be goin' for a ride."

Willard, about to say that he didn't care how they achieved the goal, stopped when Connors stood, dropped her towel, and as if ignoring him, casually sat down at the water's edge and then slipped into the pool. He had never had an ulcer, but was becoming convinced that continued exposure to the apathy, disrespect, and insolence of these people would eventually give him one.

"Well," he said, pain in his voice, "that's all I have to say. Other particulars are in the folder, Mary, so take a look and make your plans. . . . You won't be able to hit them in the airport, of course, but after that, well, you're on your own. And yes, Ms. Henry, your motorcycle might prove quite useful."

Then he and George stood, as did Maggie and Coldgrave.

"Thanks for coming," said Maggie pleasantly. "Come anytime."

With a certain incredulity in his voice, he thanked her and said they would be sure to, and then they left.

As they passed through the gateway and turned onto the highway to head back to New York, Willard said to George, "They're difficult to work with. It's like they're all crazy, but each in a different way. I can't do anything with them. . . . Did you see that magnum pointing right at us?"

Soberly, "I did, sir. It was loaded."

"They're off the charts, George, there's no other way to say it. I suppose they're useful, they get the job done, but cleaning up is, like, I have to send in a fleet of sanitation trucks. You should get clearance to see the photos taken after the state park job. Incredible. The man's head was very nearly blown completely off. The whole inside of the car was a mass of blood. You know, they don't just kill people, they kill them twice, like Packard says."

"Who hired them?"

"They were transitioned from advisors to agents by Paul Kessler. Boy, that guy was crazy, too, I think. It was a theory of his that amateurs could be more, and get this—more innovative than trained agents. The Agency not only went for it, but allowed him to add nutcases like that Packard to the team. Eventually Kessler's theory was considered proven, and voila, a crazy bunch of killers on the payroll. Talk about stupid."

With a shrug, "Have they failed?"

"Not really, except for doing things like burning the house down over the people they've butchered, and in a residential neighborhood, broad daylight, I kid you not. . . . That Connors—good grief, talk about a wraith from hell."

"Yes, sir."

"And not one of them has any respect for authority. Did you see Connors just get up and take a dip while I was talking? And you can't miss their politics—they're practically anarchists.

Bradley, he's the only one, like that Henry woman said, he's the only one with a sense of duty and country. It's unbelievable."

"What's with the Coldgrave woman?"

"Well, it's no secret, she's a bit of an alcoholic, I'm afraid. High-functioning, as they say, but yeah. Which is too bad. I mean, you saw her, George, she's beautiful. Beautiful, smart, and talented."

"Yes, sir. I agree."

"She's also obscenely rich. She has her own money, which I understand is so substantial that it probably cannot be counted. The family she comes from is so rich that there's no point talking about it."

With a grin, "So, what's wrong with her?"

With a sigh, "A lot, George, believe me. She's kind of a piece of work."

"Messed up in her mind?"

"I don't know if I'd put it that way. But she's very strange, in many ways stranger than the others. I guess a better term would be *unique.* She's unique even among the strange. Unique in a negative sense, you understand."

"How so?"

"Well, for one thing, she comes across as refined, somewhat sensitive, you might say. But actually she can be quite brutal. I'm not sure she has any meaningful sense of the value of human life. And, George, she's brutal—a real dragon."

CHAPTER 15

Philadelphia International Airport, August

"I've got them," said Coldgrave into the phone, "I'm walking behind them, about fifty feet. Blue shirt, red shirt, ball caps."

Even as she closed the phone, keeping her eye on the two men, she heard the motorcycle as Bobbie Lee and Connors rumbled past her. They would loop the parking garages and come through again. She followed the men for a good distance, finally arriving at the car rentals area. Then she crossed the roadway and stood watching them from the other side. Finally she opened the phone and texted both Connors and Bradley, *White ford van leaving now.*

Half a minute later, the motorcycle, which had looped, passed her again, its engine roaring, heading toward the freeway. Within seconds, the SUV stopped in front of her.

"Go, go," she said, climbing in. "They're headed for 95 South."

Nearly a minute had passed when Bradley said, "There's the bike, and I see the van too. Looks like we've got them."

From under her seat she retrieved the 686 and laid it on her lap. From the glove compartment she grabbed two speed-loaders and placed them beside her on the seat. Then she released the seatbelt, turned sideways, and put the window down.

Bradley, who had been accelerating, exclaimed, "Yes!" as they closed on the motorcycle. "We're at seventy-five now. They're closing on the van, see? Good grief, this is too much traffic, they can't do it here. They're crazy, they're nuts."

But even as he spoke, her hand tightened upon the magnum's grip. "Close in," she ordered, her back to him, the gun ready to be thrust out, "close in now!"

Instantly he shoved the accelerator down, and they began to close the gap faster upon the motorcycle. Now directly behind the Harley, they saw Connors pull the magnum as Bobbie Lee gave a final twist to the throttle, sending them up to the rear left window of the van.

"Go now!" ordered Coldgrave. "Get up beside them. Now! Now!"

Bradley floored it, pulling to the left of the roaring bike. Then Connors touched Bobbie Lee's shoulder and they shot up beside the driver's window. Bradley did the same, to the left of the motorcycle. Coldgrave, ready, two hands on the gun, waited for Connors to act.

"There's too damn much traffic," said Bradley, checking his mirror and noting a car racing past on his left. "Hey, that guy's speeding."

An instant later, Connors acted, leveling the big gun and firing into the glass, first at the driver's head, then at the other man, quickly dumping all seven shots of the 686. Coldgrave then thrust the gun out and sent her seven shots into the side of the driver's door, just missing Connors. Switching the .357 to her left hand, Connors yanked the .38 from under her shirt and held it out ready as Bobbie Lee moved them right up next to the driver's window. But alredy the vehicle had begun to veer to the right, so Bobbie Lee backed off, pulling them up behind it. Bradley did the same, to follow the motorcycle. The veering of the van, only slight at first, suddenly sent it toward the guardrail. Following a terrific crunch and spin, the vehicle flipped out onto the roadway, where it slid on its side, producing a spray of sparks and metal and glass debris.

Bobbie Lee, avoiding the debris, stopped the bike beside the top of the van, which lay on its side, emitting steam like a sewer vent. Connors, off before the kickstand was out, ran to the front and began firing in through the windshield. Bradley stopped just behind the bike, and both he and Coldgrave got out and followed Bobbie Lee to where Connors stood. She looked at them just as there was a double pop, dropping her. As Bobbie Lee threw herself over Connors and began firing the P-64 in through the blown-in windshield, Bradley and Coldgrave began firing into the van's top.

"God fuckin' dammit!" yelled Connors, both hands tight upon her thigh. "Fuckin' paece o' shet!"

Bobbie Lee got up, shoved a fresh mag home, and reaching in through the glassless front, put three shots into each man's head. Bradley followed this by doing the same with his 1911.

"Get her into the back seat," ordered Coldgrave, putting her free hand under Connors' arm.

Bradley, who had gotten in through the back of the van, was now rummaging inside for the computers. All around them cars began to accumulate at the shoulder of the highway and people to get out. Once inside, Connors again gripped the bleeding leg, as the entire thigh area of her jeans was dark with blood.

When a woman holding a cell phone approached, Coldgrave, gripping the magnum loosely with her right hand, held her left hand out flat for her to halt. "Don't," she said firmly. "There's been an accident, go back to your car—now."

But Connors called to the woman from her open door, "Hey, lady, gat me gun, would you? Et's a .38."

Coldgrave said she would get it, instead, and again ordered the woman back to her car. Eyeing the magnum and the bloodied Connors, the woman simply turned and walked away. After retrieving the dropped gun, Coldgrave got in beside Connors and pulled the door shut.

"Just keep pressure on it," she said.

Then Bradley emerged from the van with two laptops. He got in, dropped the shift, and accelerated, even as the motorcycle tore away, it's exhaust blatting. But then it slowed and soon pulled in behind the SUV.

"She's still bleeding," said Coldgrave, lifting her hands from Connors' leg.

"I'm already looking for an exit," he returned. "We'll take her back to HUP."

The Estate

For Connors, hobbling around on crutches was frustrating to the point of being ridiculous. But she did not laugh, for the pain in her leg often grew to an intensity that even restricted her to bed or a wheelchair. Worse, she had been forbidden by the surgeon to drink alcohol while on the prescribed medications, which made no sense to her, as the painkillers seemed only mildly effective. She warned that without the additional sedation of Irish whiskey, or some such, she would be liable to swear.

But she had been through it many times and took consolation in knowing that eventually the wound would heal and the hole close up and scar over, leaving her to get on with life. She had been fortunate, for she had been shot at close range and could easily have been killed. She was not given to philosophizing, but did admit that it was better to be stitched up by a surgeon than dressed up by a mortician. So, yes, she did want to get on with life, even in the business of death. Besides, she had found a friend, a spirit like her own, in Bobbie Lee, someone who could anticipate her mind and understand her heart.

The team had again been told to rest and take a vacation. But Willard had not been happy with the project. He would never accept casualties, he said, no matter how light. Even if Connors and Bobbie

Lee required risk to keep them interested in the work, still Connors herself was now incapacitated and could have been killed. He made the further point that more times than not the team's own methods necessarily led to a significant increase in risk. He questioned why every target must be engaged at close range, and suggested the team back off and engage a target from a safer distance. But in the end his suggestions were rejected so soundly by Connors, Bobbie Lee, and Coldgrave that he simply withdrew them.

By the end of September, the leisure life around the pool had ceased, for the weather had brought cool days and cold nights. In early October the pool was again covered and made secure.

Nearly every weekend, Coldgrave got the Bentley out and drove to New York. Parties, she said, especially seasonal parties, were part of who she had always been and who she still was. On one such outing she invited Gretchin to go along. They left early Friday morning and did not return until very late Sunday evening. For Coldgrave it had been simply another weekend to be with family and friends, a time to relax and recharge her batteries, as she said. For Gretchin, it had been a time of intrigue and excitement, an opportunity to look into the world of opulence. She said she had been able to sit and chat with the rich all day, but not able to match their capacity for alcohol.

Coldgrave was not the only one who needed to get away. Bradley too required what he called personal time, making trips into Philadelphia to do the rounds and reconnect with buddies he had kept in touch with. If Gretchin accompanied him, she would have him drop her off near her old studio, where she might walk familiar streets, visit a favorite restaurant, or drop in at an old haunt. Even Maggie would occasionally have Packard take her back to visit with friends in the old Lawncrest neighborhood. As for Packard himself, who claimed he had never had any friends, not much was required in the area of nostalgia. He was, as Maggie often put it, with her own special touch of dark humor, just not the sentimental kind.

CHAPTER 16

At Thanksgiving Willard, along with George, came again. Presenting cranberry sauce that he himself had made, he casually tossed his coat over a chair, as though he had come home. The cavalier in his attitude was so like that of a college student on holiday that Maggie asked if he had brought his dirty laundry. But he only laughed as she hung up the coat.

But concerns that he had brought his intrusiveness with him ran deep. Aside, Maggie commented to Gretchin that once someone, anyone, especially someone from the Agency, put his nose into your personal affairs, you could count on its staying there. His nose, she added, was in the door. But Gretchin, more suspicious, said the rat had stuck its nose all the way into the pantry.

"Another great meal," Willard said, smacking his lips and giving each of them an earnest look. "Thanksgiving is a very national holiday." And with a quick glance at Packard, then Coldgrave,

"Very diverse, with everyone included. And Native Americans too. That's how it started, right? Wonderful."

"That's so good of you," said Gretchin, "to include the injuns."

What had he done? What was it with her that every time he gave out sugar to her ear he got back sand in his face? "I'm sorry," he replied, "but inclusiveness is quite popular now. There's nothing wrong with that, Gretchin, and could you please pass the corn?"

"Well, these days," she returned, handing him the warm bowl, "inclusiveness simply means condescension."

"What do you mean by *these days*?"

"I mean," she replied indignantly, "I mean that, these days, as opposed to at other times in history, everyone's so goddamn phony as to make anything they say useless. What do you think I mean?"

He frowned and looked down at his plate. "That's a little negative, don't you think, especially since this should be a positive time?"

"Not much of what is generally believed about this Turkey Day of yours is actually true. But it's, like, who could even eat apple pie anymore without all the bullshit defining it?"

Maggie groaned. "I didn't need that image, Gretchin, especially since I made the pie."

"But," said Willard, looking straight at Gretchin, "that's true of everything. There are still the core truths, though, don't you think? We may not go for George Washington not being able to tell a lie, but he was a good man and a great president."

"Personally," she returned, "I don't think there's such a thing as a great president."

"And you would rank the current president where?"

"Right up there at the bottom, with all the rest of them."

"Weird," he said, with a shake of his head. After offering the observation that there was certainly room in American politics for everybody's opinion, he cut into his ham and queried Packard why he felt it necessary to bring his magnums to the table. Packard's response that it was because his shotgun seemed too big induced Willard to give George a see-what-I-mean look and then to say to everyone, "You people sure do know how to burn a guy's fuse. But this is America, right? And as Americans we want to support the system."

"Meaning what," retorted Packard, "that we keep our finger outside the trigger guard, that we're careful to come across as TV cops and that we're safe?"

"A little sensitivity and safety isn't harmful," said Willard. "Without them, one comes across as, well, crass, maybe stupid. There are three hundred million of us here now, Mr. Packard." And without waiting for a response, he looked at George, who seemed interested only in his turkey and coleslaw, and said, "George here is sensitive and safe, right, George? He's a consumer—ha."

Since a grin from George would have been inappropriate, as his mouth was full, Connors took the opportunity to say that safe and sensitive people couldn't get the fucking job done, as they were anemic.

Meeting the colorless eyes, Willard pictured her yanking the gun from her bra, then psychotically executing someone with it. Instinctively turning away, he asked Bobbie Lee if she might pass the teapot. After filling his cup, he cast a glance in the direction of Tai Ping. What a monster, sleeping in his chair like that, a kind of troll at the gate. He wasn't just a dog, a pet, a mere mammal, he was a reptile like every other creature in the household. Ah, *creature*, that term was a stretch. God himself made monsters, but who made these people, these reptiles? They seemed to have no conscience, no morals whatever. Although, to be honest, he had to admit that each of them seemed to have his or her, or indeed its, own brand of morality. But certainly it was not any kind of morality one could sell these days, especially at Thanksgiving.

Late in the afternoon, when the sun was falling fast, throwing its amber shafts across the Estate, Willard, setting his cup upon the tea cart, opened a folder and began to give the background and basic details of a new project.

"A man and a woman," he said, "two very dangerous people, rather mercilessly, we might say, took the lives of two of our agents working in the Middle East."

"*Mercilessly?*" said Gretchin. "That's how *we* do things—everyone on the team. Why do you have to introduce morality into it?"

He was firm. "Because it belongs."

"Oh, so, I'm supposed to show mercy when I blow someone's brains out?"

"No, Gretchin," he returned, "I'm not saying that. But after all, you have to admit, we are the merciful side."

"Oh, my God," she uttered, with a shake of her head. "Did you ever shoot somebody at close range? I mean, right up close, like—*that*—you know, like, *Bang!* Did you ever do that? Because I did. I tricked him into taking me for a ride, and then, just like that, wham, wham, wham, whatever, blood all over the goddamn car and all over me too. If I was going to show him mercy, at least I might have explained things to him first."

He stared at her for this.

But Coldgrave said, "We know what you're saying, Gretchin. Bob, I think, simply wants to tell us about the project. Please let him continue."

"No!" she shot back. "No fucking way. You tell him," and here she pointed at him, "to keep his wretched mercy out of this, don't even mention it, because if I ever buy into the bullshit that mercy has any place in this business, I won't be able to sleep at night—or even ever again, thank you very much."

With a sigh, Coldgrave replied, "All right, Gretchin, I do see your point. Don't get so upset. Just let it go, for now."

"No, you don't see my point," she persisted. "I don't think you see it at all." And again pointing at Willard, "I'm not going to see us as the good guys, like he wants me to. It's not a matter of good guys or bad guys, it's simply my goddamn yard as opposed to their goddamn yard, that's all. God doesn't live in my fucking yard, okay? *My* theology, anyway, says he wouldn't want to live in either yard."

"All right, all right," she returned, exasperated. "You've said your say. And for the most part, I agree with you. But Bob is entitled to his opinion."

"But he's exporting his opinion. I'm not eating his self-righteous soup. I'm not doing this job with a Bible in one hand and a gun in the other, because that's what he wants."

Here Willard protested. "I didn't say that, Gretchin."

"Bullshit!" she uttered, her eyes closed, running a hand through her hair. "You implied it. You're going to have to back out of this, or I'm not going ahead with anything. I was not moral when I shot that man or anybody else, and I'm not going to let you tell me I have to think I was. I just fucking shot him, that's all. You and the Agency can keep your righteous nationalism, bud. It's just about *my yard*."

He rubbed his chin. "But you're not a mercenary, Gretchin, we don't pay you enough for that."

"Well," she replied, "let's just say I love my yard."

Then Bradley spoke up. "I see it Bob's way. I guess I'm the only one on the team who does, but for me, it's not just about my country, it's about the right country. When I look at the two sides, I see ours as the right side. And it's not just because it's my yard, as Gretchin says, it's because it's the right yard to be in. I'm a patriot, I admit it."

Willard held up a hand. "I know that, Bradley, thank you for that. I personally have to see things that way." Putting his hands together, as if deliberating, he said, "Okay, Gretchin, I'll back off. See it any way you like, that's fine. . . . So, let me go on. As to the background, it was a highly toxic situation, but let it suffice to say that our people posed no immediate threat whatever. In fact, one was a logistics manager, the other a kind of glorified typist." And as Gretchin was about to speak out again, he continued quickly, "Anyway, the targets have left a number of others behind them. This man and woman are malignant entities, no matter how you look at it."

Bobbie Lee, who clearly had had enough of the discussion, queried, flexing the muscles in her forearms, "Where are these people? And how 'bout weapons, what're we up against?"

He brightened. "Intel says probably only hand-guns, but of course, expect more. As to where they are, that's interesting, because they are actually in New York, the Bronx. But intel believes they are headed for Pittsburgh, then Philadelphia, then home to the Bronx. If they leave within twenty-four hours, you can wait for them to show in Philly, but after that you'll have to get them in New York. The window's very narrow, about two weeks max."

"You know what," put in Gretchin, "I'll bet your intel creeps watch me take a shower."

A smile. "We do watch a lot, yes. But being moral, we try not to do anything that would offend anyone."

"I'll bet."

"All right," he said, as if to bring things to a close, "here's the packet. The guy's a blond, the girl's a blond, both very recognizable. They have no scruples, so be careful. They'll easily kill any of the public they can grab for a hostage. . . . Well, George, what say we get on the road?"

"Yes, sir."

But Willard sat for a moment, as if contemplating, then said, "Gretchin, if I may, I'd like to ask you a question." At this, of course, every eye went to him. "If you're not after what's right in life, what exactly are you after?"

She also took a moment, then answered, "What am I after? To die comfortable, not uncomfortable like Martina, in the stifling heat. Just the opposite, I think."

"But she also died in honor. Isn't that important, too?"

"No, not so much," she replied. "You can keep your honor, I'll just take the winter."

He looked at her, letting his hands fall upon his knees. With his shoulders bent, he stood, and waited for George to get up. Then they both left.

CHAPTER 17

Philadelphia, December

"Anything from Kelly?" queried Coldgrave as she looked across the table at Bradley. With a gloved hand she lifted the glass and took a few pulls at the dark beer.

He watched as she swallowed, then answered, "Nothing. I'll let you know, trust me."

"No," she returned, "I will not trust you."

He looked at the rich, cognac-colored shooting gloves, recalling how she had killed the man in the rain. Then he lifted his beer and drank. When his phone buzzed, he opened it, read the text, and said, "She says they're in the city, heading east on Pine."

"Tell them to keep circling close to Rittenhouse Square."

"Okay." And putting down the beer, he tapped out, *At a pub. Heading for ritt sq on foot. You keep circling close to sq.*

Gretchin gave a sniff. "We should've gotten something to eat, my stomach's too empty for just beer."

But two minutes later the three were making their way along Locust toward the Square. After crossing at 18th, they split, with Bradley going left, and Gretchin right. Coldgrave took a position near the fence to keep watch. She kept the phone in her coat pocket, as it was very cold out. In the other pocket she gripped the 642. Across the street at the corner restaurant most patrons were choosing to eat inside, despite the presence of propane-fired sidewalk heaters.

At Walnut and 18th Gretchin headed into the park, while at Locust and 18th Bradley did the same. Hopefully the intel prediction that the targets would show up in center city would prove correct.

Then Coldgrave's phone buzzed, with the text from Connors reading, *Nothing so far. Circling park now. By the church.* She heard the motorcycle as it rounded the far corner of the Square and headed for 18th. As they rumbled past her she nodded to them to keep up the search. Soon Bradley, who had met up with Gretchin at the park's center, texted, *Nothing. Heading out. See you soon.*

It was then that Coldgrave looked up. From the entrance of the Park Restaurant across the street, stepped two women followed by two men. Opening the phone she texted Connors and Bradley, *I have them. Caution. Others with them.* Within moments Gretchin and Bradley were standing beside her and the motorcycle had come to an idle at the curb across the street.

"They're heading north on 18th," she said, opening the phone. "Keep them in view, follow them, we'll be right behind you." As they left, she crossed the street. Bobbie Lee sent a quick rev to the chugging motor, while Connors seemed to look longingly toward the restaurant. "They have another couple with them. I'm calling Willard."

Bobbie Lee rolled her eyes at the mention of Willard's name, but Connors, her face expressionless, merely reached into the pocket of her heavy leather jacket and closed her hand on the .38.

"Hi, Bob. . . . Listen, we've found them, but they're with another couple, about the same age. They look like friends or whatever. There are a significant number of people around, even though it's pretty cold out. . . . Yes, Gretchin and Bradley are following them, and the motorcycle is ready to go. . . . Right. Okay, surely. . . . Surely. . . . Look, it's your timetable, you tell me. . . . Well, personally, I'd go for it. . . . Yes, right here on the street. But I'm listening, so what's your decision? . . . Okay, we'll do that. . . . Bye."

"What'd he say?" queried Connors, her eyes following Gretchin and Bradley.

"He said to go for it. We can follow them a little, but he said don't let them get into a residential neighborhood or go into a house. You guys get up close to Gretchin and Bradley, but let them do it."

Turning, she crossed to the other corner and while putting the call through to Gretchin, launched into a brisk walk. Then pocketing the phone, she heard the motorcycle at her flank. Now she saw Gretchin put her hand on Bradley's arm and give him the orders, and then she saw both deglove and put their hands into their pockets, their pace quickening.

Turning into a side street, Coldgrave pressed the key, then entered the SUV and started it. Unlocking all the doors, she checked her mirror and pulled away from the meter. Making a right onto 18th, she lowered her speed. With Bradley and Gretchin in view, she slowed to a creep, her eye taking in the number of pedestrians. Ahead she saw the motorcycle, now behind Bradley on his flank. Carefully she brought the SUV up close behind the Harley. The two targets with their companions were a mere five to eight feet ahead of Bradley and Gretchin.

Suddenly Gretchin, who also had been moni-toring the pedestrian traffic, looked over her shoulder, gave a little wave to Bobbie Lee, then to Coldgrave, then faced forward. Without further warning, she touched Bradley's arm again. She pulled the 9 mm even as he the .45, and they both stepped quickly forward and put the weapons to the backs of the targets and fired twice. Instantly the targets collapsed onto the sidewalk. Their companions, recoiling, began to yell and screech, then, their faces an awful rose color, simply took off running. Bradley leveled the .45 down at his target's head and fired, blasting a massive hole and tearing most of the man's ear away. Gretchin did the same, firing into her target's head, blowing the woman's cap off. Then repocketing, they turned and walked back, past the motorcycle, to the SUV and got in.

Coldgrave watched as the motorcycle then accelerated, made a left, and was gone. Two women, who had come from a dress shop across the street, were still standing where they had watched the entire attack. A man, who had halted his progress along the sidewalk when the shooting commenced, still stood with his mouth open. There were others too who had chosen not to run, but to witness everything. After checking her mirror, Coldgrave slowly accelerated, then took the first available right.

The Estate

As the dining room fireplace seemed to be providing more heat than usual, Packard turned the thermostat up in the hallway to ensure warmth throughout the house. Opening the front door, he looked out for the arrival of the returning vehicles. The first to make its way up the drive and toward the stables was the Harley. Both riders had their visors down. Close behind was the SUV. Not bothering with a coat, he opened the door and went out.

Later, with everyone seated at the dining room table, Maggie brought in apple pie and tea and coffee. If she did not naturally possess a serving temperament, she did possess a pastoral one. "Fresh apple pie," she announced, "and if you don't want tea or coffee, I can get you something cold, so speak up."

"Tae sounds good," said Connors, still rubbing the cold from her knuckles.

"That's tea, not tae, girl," said Bobbie Lee, giving Connors a nudge. "You oughta work on that." And when Connors in response gave her the finger, she said, "Boy, the road's a mess out there. I have no doubt it was that Virgin Mary of yours that got us home safe. You'd better git the rosary out and git to thankin' her."

Gretchin poured tea into her cup, then reached for the pie plates. "Thanks, Len, for the nice hot fire. It is cozy—ah."

"Yeah," agreed Bradley, after indicating he wished the coffee passed, "it's almost hot in here."

"Hotter'n it is for them two on the sidewalk," quipped Bobbie Lee. "Or I guess not, given their bent. But, Gritchin, me'n Killy're sure glad you guys took the job today, since her lig's a-killin' her."

Gretchin's eyebrows went up. "I suppose it's getting easier for me."

"Bob thinks so," said Bradley, "and I do, too."

"Bradley," she returned, "don't refer to him, please. That guy makes me so mad."

"Ah, come on, he's okay. You just need to roll with it a little more. Don't let him get to you, he's a good guy."

Coldgrave, lifted her cup, "This is certainly excellent pie, Maggie, many thanks. Very nice."

"Know somethin'?" said Bobbie Lee. "I'd sure hate to work on one of the Agency's cleanup crews, with the mess today, in front of ever'body. Whew."

Connors slurped her tea, then replied, "Et wasn't bad today, the bodies probably half froze before they got there, at laest the blood ded."

"Yeah," returned Bobbie Lee, "but what if it was in the summer? Guess they jist wash all the blood 'n shit down the sewer."

"All right," put in Maggie, clearly uncomfortable, "you're all here, that's what I care about."

Connors winced. "I've stell got a hole in me lag."

"Well," said Maggie, "thankfully we're all together."

Packard shifted in his chair. "Thankfully, dear?"

"And why not?"

"Because I get enough of that from Willard," he grunted.

"You don't really think, Lenny," she said, "that your safety depends just on your prowess, do you? You can't really think that."

"No, I don't." he returned. "But since I can't determine what it does depend on, why's it matter? Maybe it's a combination of things, or just luck. Who cares? I don't care why I'm safe, just *that* I'm safe. And if I was dead, I wouldn't care about that."

"Agreed," said Bobbie Lee, tapping the table with her spoon. "Give me realism every time."

"Spaekin' of rael," said Connors, "I t'ink we should gat oursalves a car and put the motorcycle away untel spreng."

Making a face, "I'm the one that takes the wind."

"All right," said Coldgrave, "I am going to bed early, I think. Good night, everyone. I do thank you all so much for an efficiently executed project. It was delightful. Good night, now. Maggie, I think I'll take a little ice up with me."

The good night was returned, and they watched as she slid her chair out, went to the kitchen with Maggie, returned with a glass of party ice, and then left the room. But Gretchin watched Bradley as he followed Coldgrave with his eyes. It was, she considered, pathetic what men possessed, a dick, a gun, a car, and sometimes, like this man, a country, but not much more. And what more was there for this man? Did he want Mary or herself?

CHAPTER 18

In her room, Coldgrave set the glass down on the marble-topped dresser and took her shoes off. They were not highheels, of course, for she may have needed to run. After going to the bathroom and brushing her teeth, she took another glass, of clearest lead crystal, put some ice in it, and looked over the array of liquors on the dresser. Choosing the Sapphire, she filled half the glass with gin and sat down before the mirror.

"That's a nice face," she said aloud. "If I were in need of a face, I might choose that one." Taking a drink from the glass and letting the magic liquid roll over her tongue, then swallowing it with utter satisfaction, she continued, "Except for the wayward eye."

After draining the glass, she added ice and poured herself another. Life was like a dream. It was perhaps real, but it was so very much like a dream, like a glass of gin. Certainly it did not taste as good as gin. Putting the glass to her nose, she took in the subtle combination of aromas. Could she detect the juniper berries or not? Well, perhaps mixed with lipstick. Her eye went to the lips in the mirror, then the nose, then the eyes. It all looked like her own face, but then, life was like that—it played with you until you didn't know your own face from that of someone else, or even until you didn't know yourself from yourself.

Later, when she was in bed and had pulled the covers up, she looked up at the photograph and into the face of the girl by the pool with her dog. Since Bopo and the swimming pool had been real, why hadn't the girl been real?

As serious cold moved in, pouring through the trees and over the whitened yards, the Estate took on its usual winter persona. Christmas was had, as was New Year's. January swaggered like a beast, so that Bradley and Packard were forced to affix the old wooden shutters from the stable. Wood was delivered for the fireplace, as Bradley, fearing he might strain his shooting arm, had not wanted to split logs. But Packard grumbled at using the fireplace at all, citing common knowledge of the inefficiency of such a contraption. Hell, a fireplace took the very same heat the furnace produced and practically blew it up the chimney, as if to heat the outside air! So, why would anyone want one, except for popping corn or toasting one's toes? But Maggie, Gretchin, Connors, and Bobbie Lee said those were just the things they had in mind.

Despite the cold weather, the one activity consistently engaged in was gun practice. Packard made sure to have both the safety room and the range heated before practice began each day, priding himself in always showing an interest in the advancement of the team's shooting skills. Evenings found him reading gunsmithing books or watching weapons videos. Maggie did not complain of this aspect of his gun obsession, grateful that after such a dark past he could be content with filling his retirement years with what she called the benign side of the shooting world.

Although Connors' leg was healing well, she could not be talked into riding out for a winter camping trip with Bobbie Lee. The hollow-point bullet's mass had missed the bone but also expanded enough to tear a huge hole through the thigh muscle. The surgeon said that with time the body would fill in the hole and bring the usability of the leg back to a reasonable level, but also that the recovery would be painful. Connors' walk became marked with a distinct limp. For her own part, she cared neither about the limp nor the appearance of another scar. She refused to see a plastic surgeon, declaring that one more scar couldn't matter. She also refused physical therapy, telling the nurse who called for making the appointment that the ride to the office would hurt too fucking much to make it worthwhile. She would try instead, she said, a little exercise and a lot of whiskey.

But if the dark months passed slowly, and were sometimes replete with boredom, they also hosted times of happiness for everyone. Many evenings were spent around a card game or at the pool table, or indeed eating popcorn and toasting one's toes at the hearth. During such times the team could easily have been mistaken for a normal, closely knit family.

It was not until spring that Willard came again for an official visit. On a Saturday morning in May he and George sat upon the couch eating chocolate chip cookies and sipping dark English breakfast tea.

"Gracious, this is good, Maggie," he declared. "Don't you think so, George? And where in the world did you get this tea? It's like nothing I've tasted before."

"Well, thank you, Bob," returned Maggie. "It's my own blend of a few loose teas I get from local markets and one from the Reading Terminal Market in Philadelphia. Glad you like it."

Again he sipped the tea, nodding to express his appreciation of its deep flavor and watching as she moved about with the teapot. He knew of the close relationship she had had with Martina. Did she know that Mary had refused his suggestion to send in a sniping unit? Did she know that Mary's insistance upon sending in an up-close team had resulted at least obliquely in Martina's death? He took another bite of cookie and let his eyes move over the rest of the team as they sat and chatted happily.

Finally, after Connors had limped in to take a seat beside Bobbie Lee, Coldgrave cleared her throat, as if to attract attention at a garden party. "Now, if everyone is happy, please give us your attention. Bob?"

As if through the power of suggestion, Willard himself cleared his throat. "Yes, thank you, Mary.

Well, everyone, how glad I am to be with you again."

Gretchin also cleared her throat. "Please don't be phony," she said. "I don't think I'm up for it. Please talk to us like we're people."

Hesitating and turning somewhat pink, "Of course, Gretchin, thank you for reminding me—we're in a family here. Okay, well, I do want to find out how you guys made it through the winter. Wow, it was a chilly one, wasn't it?"

"We didn't," replied Gretchin, "we died and went to heaven."

Ignoring this, he queried, "Are there concerns from anyone about the team before I present a new project? Any complaints?"

"Me lag hurts," said Connors.

"Yes, well, I would think it might. Is therapy coming along well?"

"Haven't taken et."

"Why, if it hurts, may I ask?"

"Don't loike doctors."

"I understand, Kelly," he said. "Not fond of them myself. What do you do when it hurts, then, may I ask?"

"Drenk and take me gun to the range."

His eyes went closed. "Yes, and does that help?"

"Hell fuckin' no, not much."

"Yes, well, . . . so, anybody else, any other complaints or comments?" After a pause, he continued, "I wanted to thank everyone for a job well done on the last project. There were no casualties and cleanup wasn't too bad. There were a lot of witnesses and subsequent complaints, as you might understand. But then, I was the one who gave the go-ahead for doing it on the street, wasn't I? Anyway, no harm done. Now, let's go on. I have a new project, one I think you'll find interesting. The Russians, it seems, are back in the spy game." And chuckling, "Little joke there."

Gretchin put her hands to her cheeks melodramatically. "Yeah, funny, Bob, and do you do impressions?"

Forcing his anger into submission, as even George had let out a snicker, he continued, "So, with Crimea and now Ukraine, the Russians are stepping up their activity here in the U.S. We've caught so many of their agents that, frankly, we don't know what to do with them. They've caught a few of ours, of course. But only a few, since our activity isn't nearly as much as theirs."

"Right," shot Gretchin sarcastically, "because they're more deceptive and conniving, sure."

"Yes, I think they are," he retorted indignantly. "But in any case, we have caught a good many of their agents. Oh, and I don't mean mere infiltrators, like Osipov. No Anna Chapman stuff here, I mean real agents." Here, sensing he had inadvertently crossed a line, he halted, then said, "I don't mean to say that Stanley Osipov wasn't a great guy, he was for sure, a really great guy, of much help to the Agency. But anyway, the Russians now want these agents back, as we do ours, and a trade is on."

Bradley, playing with his shoestring, said, "Yeah, but they're really crooked, everybody knows that. I never thought Osipov was genuinely on our side."

"How so, Mr. Hopkins?"

"I don't know, really. I never saw proof or anything, it's just that he had been a spy for the other side. Why did Martina even fall for him anyway?"

Gretchin, her brow furrowing, said, "Be careful, Bradley."

"What's that supposed to mean?"

"I mean, Bradley boy, that we all liked him, all of us except for you. And if you keep running your mouth just because he isn't here, you're going to get on worse than our bad side."

Giving her a look, "That's a veiled threat."

"Veiled?"

"All right, then, a threat."

Bobbie Lee said with a smirk, "Well, look at that, girls, maybe he isn't stupid after all."

Ignoring this, Bradley said, "You heard it, Bob—a threat."

Willard lifted his chin. "Gretchin, Bradley's right, we have to be judicious in what we say to each other and about each other."

Looking at Willard, then at Bradley, she said, "Drop dead, both of you."

He had learned that it was not possible to best this woman by coming up with the last quip. "So, let me finish about the project, if I may. I said trade, but it gets tricky. The Russians have two of our agents, we have eight of theirs."

"Oh," she put in, "so, six of ours are still sneaking about Moscow with their goddamn little cameras?"

He gave her a cold stare, then continued. "We're willing to make an even swap, obviously since two of ours are worth eight of theirs. But it gets sticky. Unfortunately one of our agents was caught propositioning a minor. The girl's mother actually turned him in. More unfortunately, the local Russian police decided to shoot him on the way to the police station."

With solemnity, Bradley said, "I guess we want the body?"

A sigh. "Yes, we do, but the Agency believes the orders to kill him came from the FSB."

Grinning. "The KGB?"

"That's not an acceptable term, Mr. Hopkins. I'm sure you know that."

He shrugged. "Just joking, like Gretchin does."

"Anyway, with the Crimea and Ukraine situations being rather unmanageable, the Agency feels it is imperative that we respond, so to speak, in kind. In short, two of their agents have to be put down before the swap." And with a little shrug, "It's a message. Retaliatory force is all they understand, I'm afraid."

Bradley frowned. "Just two?"

Impatiently, "Yes, just two. I didn't make the decision."

Another frown. "But if two are worth eight, why wouldn't one be worth four?"

"I just said two. Is that all right with you, Mr. Hopkins? Besides, the team will not be involved with these Russian agents. I've simply filled you in on some of the background so you'll know what it's all about."

Bradley smiled. "Sure, Bob. I was only doing the math."

"Arithmetic," corrected Gretchin. "Bradley doesn't do math."

"This is," continued Willard, rubbing his neck, "where the team gets involved. I've given you the background to the swap, as it impacts upon your part in the operation. Your targets will actually be three other individuals, extremely dangerous entities, who are bent upon ruining negotiations between Russia and the U.S."

"I thought that was the news media's job," quipped Gretchin.

He gave the bridge of his nose a scratch, as if to express his annoyance with her interruptions. Then he simply continued, "The targets are patriotic Russians who loathe any kind of positivity in the relationship of the two countries. They've killed many times in order to disrupt negotiations. Neither we nor the FSB has been able to stop them yet. This will be your job. The FSB has given us a tip, amazingly, that these guys are in the U.S., and has asked us to arrest them. We're not going to do that, we're going to kill them. And that will be your job."

Then Maggie asked, "What happens if the Russians pull out of the swap deal after you put down their two agents?"

He smiled. "They could very well do that—just keep our guy and wait for another deal. Or obviously they could shoot him to make it even, two for two." He shrugged. "One of the problems with this work, as I'm sure you've figured out, is that everyone in it is ultimately expendable. It's the nature of the beast, I'm afraid."

She looked at him for a moment, but then said, "I'm sure you're right, but I meant, should we then step down on the project?"

"Oh. Good question. The answer is a definitive no, execute it anyway. These three disruptors have been a thorn in everybody's rear end. We cannot miss this opportunity to eliminate them. Tips like this are rare from the FSB. So, we're not going to play games with this one, we're going to hand them three heads. Again, I only gave you the background so you would know what drives these three individuals, and that they are very, very driven."

He looked around at them, but paused at Coldgrave, who had given the ice in her glass a shake. He watched as she tipped the glass up. Why would any woman so beautiful want to drink so much? Beautiful, talented, intelligent, rich—what a waste. Maybe she couldn't fall in love or didn't know who to fall in love with. So many times had he imagined going out with her.

Bobbie Lee then queried, "Where are these guys, and what kind of stuff do they carry?"

"They're in Washington, D.C., actually, where the swap is to take place. Since getting the tip we've gathered substantial intel, even clear photos. It's all in this packet."

"When?" she queried further.

"Middle of June should be just about perfect. Negotiations are ongoing, but the swap is tentatively scheduled for July. . . . Try to make it quick. They're in a rented apartment, but going in on these people will probably result in casualties. As usual, a standoff is out of the question. The street would be great. You seem to be especially good at that."

CHAPTER 19

Washington, D.C., June 2015

At the next corner, Bradley took the SUV right. He marveled that Coldgrave could be so calm, almost serene, like some kind of guru, so that the sound of her phone snapping shut seemed mundane, even silly. From the back seat came the click of Gretchin's magazine going home.

"Any word?" he queried.

Coldgrave slid her sunglasses on. "No," she answered. "And don't keep asking me."

He should not have asked. He knew they were simply to keep moving through the neighborhood until the woman called. In his mirror he could see the motorcycle, even Bobbie Lee's eyes and part of Connors' hair as it protruded like angel feathers from under her helmet. Then he heard the phone vibrate.

Coldgrave opened it. "Hi, yes. . . . Yes. . . . White, okay. . . . Uh, two turns and we're there. . . . Surely. . . . What are they wearing? . . . Okay, thanks. Bye." Then quickly she called Connors. "Kelly, intel called. Targets leaving now for a white minivan at the corner lot. One's in a green, one in a blue, the other in a rust-colored sport shirt. . . . I'd say about two minutes. . . . Yes. I'll call if it's a go. Stay close. . . . Bye."

The SUV made another turn and after two blocks pulled to the curb beside the parking lot. The motorcycle did the same.

"Anybody see a plain white Sienna?" Coldgrave asked.

Bradley cleared his throat. "We would have said, Mary."

"Right. Sorry." Then her phone buzzed again. "Yes? . . . Thanks, Kelly. . . . Uh-huh. . . . Bye." Then she said, pointing, "Far end of the lot, right over there."

"I see it," said Bradley, pulling the shift and accelerating as the van left the lot. He checked his mirror for the motorcycle, then followed the van around a corner and looked for an opportunity to get closer. "I'm not sure they're all in there," he said, now a mere fifty feet behind them.

But Coldgrave said, "I see all three."

"You can see their shirts?"

"I saw the shirts," said Gretchin, "and it looked to me like green, blue, and rust. Those are the colors, right?"

Coldgrave, who had pulled the .38 from her purse, said, "Pull up, we'll take a closer look." And when he moved into the left lane, she said, "Yes, that's a definite yes."

He decelerated, then moved in again behind the minivan. "But look at all these people. There's tons of people. And look, those are kids."

Laying the gun on her lap, Coldgrave picked up the phone. "Kelly, it's a go. Keep on our tail. Follow my lead, only go in if we do. . . . Yes, soon. . . . Right. . . . Bye."

"But—" said Bradley, his eyes on the many pedestrians.

"Shut up, Bradley!" shot Gretchin. "Just drive."

Giving his head a shake, he touched the panel and rolled their windows down. Checking his rearview mirror for Bobbie Lee, he moved into the left lane again and accelerated slowly until they were alongside the minivan. Then he said, "We're all stopping, the light's turning." He stopped with one car ahead of him and two ahead of the minivan.

"All right," returned Coldgrave, throwing a glance over her right shoulder, "wedge him in when the light turns. Kelly will know what to do."

On the motorcycle, now in back of the SUV and beside the minivan, Connors put her hand on the back of Bobbie Lee's jacket bottom, ready to lift it. Bobbie Lee goosed the Harley. Neither looked over at the targets in the minivan.

But suddenly the target who was driving dropped his window and said to Connors, his eyes checking the light, which was about to turn green, "Hey, biker chick, blow me!"

Slowly Connors turned her head and looked at him. He was less than five feet away. She blinked once, then deftly lifted Bobbie Lee's jacket, yanked out the magnum, swung it over at his face and fired—*Flom! Flom!* And rising on the pegs, she turned and with both hands on the gun fired in at the other two—*Blop! Blop!* and *Blop! Blop!*"

"Oh no," uttered Bradley, his eyes on the mirror.

But already Coldgrave had reacted, opening her door, gun in hand. "Stay here for now," she said clearly, stepping toward the minivan, her gun leveled at the still form of the driver.

Connors, handing the magnum to Bobbie Lee, dismounted the bike and pulled the .38 from the flash bra. The only movement inside now was from the man in the back seat, who, blood sputtering from his mouth, which had been half blown away, writhed frantically, as if trying to get out of his seatbelt. Thrusting the gun at him, she fired into his head, knocking him down upon the seat, then fired again.

Immediately Coldgrave fired into the mangled head of the dead driver, which hung forward and dripped, for the seatbelt's shoulder strap held the body upright. Then she emptied the gun into the limp man next to him.

Both women could hear screams and yells from people on the sidewalks, for all had halted at the awful scene, although some had begun to run away. Connors, nearly pushing Coldgrave aside, shoved her gun up close to the driver's ghastly head and said, "No, fucker, you blow me." Then she shot into his temple three times.

Coldgrave, who had stepped back to avoid the flying blood and flesh from the up-close blasting, now turned, gun in hand, and walked to the SUV.

As Connors reholstered and climbed back onto the motorcycle, Bobbie Lee uttered, "Good Lord! You got shit all over you, girl. You're gonna wreck my jacket."

Before climbing into the SUV, Coldgrave stopped to look around her. A kind of eerie silence was falling, as the screaming and even crying from those nearby trailed off. As the motorcycle roared away the blatting from its pipe seemed to be the only significant sound she heard. Everyone nearby, across the street, some crouching, some still standing, and people in the nearby cars, all of which had stopped, were simply staring at her.

Gun in hand, she got inside and unhurriedly closed the door. After dropping the gun back into the purse, she fastened her seatbelt. Then, her eye moving over the silent onlookers, she calmly said to Bradley, "All right, drive."

The silvery highway began to darken as the rain moved in. Coldgrave pulled the mirror down and checked her lipstick. After looking at herself for a moment, she flipped it back up. She had called Connors to query what went wrong, then Willard to report the project had been successful. Now she must live with all of it, as the incoming rain promised to be impotent to wash it away.

"How's the lipstick?" asked Bradley. "You sure check it a lot."

Gretchin could not resist responding. "Bradley, come on. Please."

"What?" he returned, finding her in his mirror. "What did I say?"

"Just don't say anything, we'll all be better off."

Coldgrave touched the corner of her mouth. "It's fine, Bradley. Not that you should be asking, of course. But it's fine."

"It's no big deal," he returned. "Conversation, right?"

Gretchin gave his seat a tap with her foot. "Men don't make conversation."

"You're saying I can't make conversation?"

"No, I'm saying you don't."

With a chuckle, "Yeah, sure. You know, if you hadn't said anything, Mary and I could have had a nice talk maybe. But you had to ruin it."

"She didn't ruin it," said Coldgrave.

With a smirk, "I think she did. And she also made me out to be typical."

"If you were any more typical, Bradley," said Gretchin, "they'd put you behind glass in a museum."

"What if I want to be nontypical."

"The term is *atypical*."

"Fine, okay, I can use that word."

"Then I would say, try being atypical, try thinking outside the simplistic perspective of your insecurity."

A chuckle. "I can do that. Look at how I accept Mary."

"Oh God! Don't, Bradley, don't say such pathetically stupid things. *Accept* her? For what?"

A quick shrug. "Well, her drinking. And she's kind of stinky rich. *I'm* not rich, *I* don't wear fancy clothes, and I sure don't own a Bentley."

But Coldgrave merely looked out her window at the wet landscape, then at the movement of the windshield wipers.

"And what's so stupid about what I say?" he continued. "You're just attacking me again. You're pathological, Gretchin, do you know that?"

"*Accept?* You *accept* her? God!"

"What's wrong with that? I'm accepting, right? That's a good thing, the last time I heard."

"You know what, Bradley? You're male, and not in a good sense. You're military, and not in a good sense. You're American, but not in a good sense. And you want to make conversation? You're the architect of your own demise in any conversation. Have you ever considered that you're the one who might need to be accepted?"

Clearing his throat to show his irritation, "Okay, blah, blah, blah. So, let's talk about something else."

With a laugh, "You've painted yourself into a corner, and you can't get out. You're uncomfortable, so you change the subject."

"I'm not uncomfortable, Gretchin, I'm very comfortable, see?" And he started to whistle.

"Just shut up, Bradley. You're such an ass. You're accepting of Mary for nothing that needs accepting. Of course, all after she saved your goddamn life in Florida. Yeah, sure, I get it—that didn't influence you at all, did it? Hell no, no fucking way! . . . Mary, what did Kelly say? What went wrong?"

Coldgrave, as if forcing herself to listen, replied, "It was difficult to hear her above the road noise, so they had to pull over. We should get a microphone installed in her helmet. It seemed like her earbuds were working okay, but I couldn't hear much. Anyway, she said something like it had seemed the right thing to do. She said she had just called it the way she saw it. So, we'll have to talk about it when we get back."

"I don't know," said Bradley, "it was pretty scary back there."

Coldgrave looked out the window again. "I understand that, Bradley."

"But you're not going to just let it go, right?"

"That's my call, not yours."

"Sure, but that was really crowded back there. You saw all those people, and the kids. I think I would've waited for a better situation."

With a sigh, "She's a good shot, Bradley, a very good shot."

Dubiously, "I don't know."

"She was perfect today."

"Bullets do crazy things. Maybe a bystander got hit and we don't know it yet."

"That's possible. But think of the destruction that most certainly would happen if we had not stopped those men."

"That sounds moral, like what Bob would say."

With another, heavier sigh, "Maybe it is, Mr. Hopkins, maybe it is."

CHAPTER 20

The Estate

"So," said Coldgrave as Maggie set the pot on the table, "tell us, Kelly, all about it, if you will. What went wrong?"

Connors took hold of the teapot and slowly filled her cup to the brim. After setting the pot in front of Bobbie Lee, she lifted her cup and softly blew over the hot liquid. "Wrong?" she repeated. "How do you mean? The fuckers are colder'n frozen shet."

"Uh, yes, but I mean as to the plan. You were to follow my lead. That didn't happen. Why?"

"A straightforward quistion," said Bobbie Lee.

"Oh, and, Kelly," added Coldgrave, "please don't play games with me. I would appreciate a candid answer."

"I like that," said Bobbie Lee, as if having fun, "a real forceful quistion."

Connors slurped the tea. "Well," she said, "me answer's t'reefold. Number one, I felt loike et.

Number two, et seemed logical. And number t'ree, yous got your carpses, dedn't yous?"

Coldgrave, who had been sitting forward, now leaned back. "Fine. But things can go very wrong that way. Ballistics being what they are, a pedestrian might have been hit by one of your bullets or fragments."

"Were they?"

"We don't know yet."

"Then, why worry about et? Joost put the carpses in bags and tow the car away. Lat et go."

Momentarily, "Actually, I'm inclined to agree with you. But let me just emphasize again, please, everybody, stick to plan, if you can. With so many factors involved, there's a reason for protocol."

Then Bradley said, "I was watching you, Kelly, and I thought he said something to you."

"He ded."

Turning his palm up, "So, what did he say?"

She looked at him. "Not your fuckin' businass."

"But," said Coldgrave, "you responded?"

"Aye, I ded."

"Well, I had made the decision to go ahead, in spite of pedestrian traffic, and I'll have to answer for any public casualties that turn up. But I was also weighing whether to abort. So, again, please don't respond like that unless you really feel you have to."

"So, you're saying," said Gretchin, "don't act independently, but if we do, you're on our side?"

"Correct. Everybody, yes?"

But the matter did not end there, for the next day Willard called to say that a bullet had indeed passed through a pedestrian's purse, just missing her and destroying an expensive smartphone. Connors merely shrugged and suggested that the Agency, after paying for the purse and smartphone, inform the woman that the alternative might have been having her phone and purse confiscated by another, much less friendly agency.

"The public," replied Coldgrave, "does not want to hear that. People only work with what they can see. Besides, you were hardly thinking such things when you opened fire."

"Who cares why the Devil is kelled, as long as the fucker's dead?"

"That smacks of moralism, to me, and you're no more a moralist than I am."

"No," agreed Connors, "but I gat offanded raeal easy."

A few weeks later Willard called Coldgrave to say that the Russians were unhappy with the deal and that negotiations had been suspended. But he seemed confident that eventually a trade would be worked out. Poker was a crazy game, he said, full of lies and evil, but at least now, because the team had removed the wild cards, it could be played without disruption.

Fortunately for Gretchin, the morning sun had already warmed the pool enough to make it easy on the toes. At sixty years of age, she had little patience left in her for enduring discomfort. Thus, she had added a jigger of vodka to her lemonade. Sitting on the side of the pool, she moved her legs luxuriously in the water and drew up more lemonade through her straw.

When Bradley came from the house with his towel and lemonade, she wondered why at a mere forty-eight he should have the slightest romantic interest in her. Yes, phenomenally her hair was still red, but not the bright red of her youth; it was graying and within a few years would no doubt be white. Her figure was full and solid, thanks to her inherited muscle structure, but still she wondered whether it was enough for this younger man. Even if it was now, within a few years it would not be. As she put her lips to the straw again, she let her eyes go shut.

"Good morning," he said cheerily, taking a seat beside her.

She put the glass down. "What time is it?"

"Ten-thirty, almost time for lunch."

"Your aviator watch?"

"Oh yeah, wouldn't be without it."

"Most people just use their phone."

"I know," he said, "but I'm not most people, which is good, right?"

"Is that the one you always swim with?"

"Yep, waterproof to a hundred meters."

"In case you hit a rain cloud?"

A chuckle. "No, in case the plane has to ditch or whatever, it's just waterproof. You didn't answer my question. Is it good I'm not like most people?" When she merely took another drink, he said, "So, you actually do think I'm typical, like you said." Again nothing. "Well, I don't think I'm typical at all, I think in some ways I'm kind of unique."

"What ways?"

"I'm interested in women older than I am, for instance, that's uncommon. And how about women with red hair, like yours? Years ago, it wasn't considered a plus to have red hair, but I've learned to overlook it."

"Anything else?" she asked, looking deep into the water.

"I can take a lot of criticism without going nuts."

"Like my criticism?"

With another chuckle, "You said it, I didn't. And that's another thing, I'm not overly critical myself. Men get critical of women."

Somehow she felt relieved to see Connors, Bobbie Lee and Coldgrave coming toward them. Bobbie Lee's red two-piece, with a sheen to it, caught her eye first, although Connors' skimpy green bikini did complement the blond hair and enhance the body scars in a striking way. Especially accentuated was the new scar on the thigh, which, unlike Bobbie Lee's from the .223, gave the appearance of a poorly healing wound from some industrial accident. She wondered if she herself would look good in such revealing swimwear. Then her eyes went to Coldgrave's one-piece, a soft, expensive-looking suit in an off-white like that of her Bentley. Its thin material seemed to show clearly every line and protuberance of the beautiful body. For some reason it gave her a sensual thrill to watch this woman walk.

Just before noon Maggie came out for a swim, along with Packard, who, helping by pushing the lunch cart, said he only wished to get a little wet. Lunch was taken poolside, leaving the rest of the afternoon open for reading and relaxation.

Toward afternoon's end, with the sun still bright but beginning to sink into the far trees, Gretchin and Bradley left to get ready for an evening of dinner and a movie in Philly. Packard closed his cleaning kit and retired to his room to enjoy, as he said, some gun smithing and whiskey in peace. Connors and Bobbie Lee stacked their magazines, pulled on sneakers, and called Helga and Tai Ping over to go for a walk. But Coldgrave and Maggie slipped into the water for a leisurely swim. Dog paddling, they moved to the center of the pool and began treading water in the luscious warmth of the falling sun.

"Oh," breathed Maggie, "could anything be so nice as this?"

Coldgrave gave her nose a delicate swipe. "I suppose this is a little piece of heaven. But if it isn't, well, who's complaining?"

"You know, Mary, I've never told you, but when we first met, when I saw you get out of your Jaguar and then walk through the door, I got the strangest feeling that you were psychic."

"What gave you that impression? Because actually I thought it about you at that time, too."

"Martina always said I was psychic. She was not one to be normal herself though. She came across as the steady, cool pragmatist, but she used to pretend she was blind. We all have our games."

"You refer to her often."

"Yes, I know I do. And I think of her often. She was the dearest person I've ever known."

"I . . . I have to tell you, Maggie, um, to a certain extent, I was responsible for Martina's death."

"Yes, because you were the contact."

Coldgrave shook her head. "No, I mean more than that. I was advised, by Bob actually, before the project to consider sending in a sniper unit instead of a close-up team. ... I didn't take the advice. Martina would still be alive, if I had only taken his advice. I think he was right and I was wrong. I'm sorry, Maggie." When there was no response, "Are you going to talk to her tonight?"

"I usually say good night to her before I go to sleep."

"Could you tell her for me that I am sorry?"

Wiping tears away with a wet hand, "I will."

CHAPTER 21

Late December

Brushing a piece of lint from his sweater, Willard looked around at the team. Vigorously his mind worked over how best to explain the Agency's rejection of his request to add another agent to the team's personnel. Today he would really be playing the bad guy. First, he had been stupid enough to request coffee in the face of Maggie's offer of tea. He couldn't repent now without appearing to be phony and pandering. Then he had said the Christmas tree was too large. Why had he done that? Now he would be handing them this. He must bolster himself, talk to them a little, be affable.

"You know," he said, raising his voice a little to effect confidence, "Maggie, I think I was wrong about that tree. I was dead wrong, it's just about perfect, I would say. Yes, it seems to fit that corner of the room very well."

"Do you think so?" she returned, looking toward the tree.

"Absolutely. I was too quick to speak. A smaller tree would look much too small for this room. Don't you think so, George?"

"Yes," replied the agent instantly. And giving the tree his consideration, he added, "I think you're exactly right, sir."

"Well," said Maggie, "I'm glad you've brought yourself to like it, Bob. Good for you."

Blinking, he then said, "Kelly, how is the leg coming along? Just about healed, is it?"

"I guess et es," she returned. "At least, I don't leak urine out the bullet hole anymore."

He closed his eyes, wishing she had not made the joke. "That's good—ha! But seriously, you didn't seem to be limping as much when you came in. I'm so glad. It could've been much worse." And turning to Bobbie Lee, "Ms. Henry, no problems healing from the Florida wound?"

"Nope."

He nodded. "Any camping trips planned for you two?"

But instead of giving him here an audible answer, Bobbie Lee merely shook her head, then deliberately turned away from him to give her attention to Connors.

He swallowed at this display of her disdain for him, but then said to her quickly, "Sure. Well, that's understandable. It's a little chilly out there for motorcycling, I guess. Okay, yeah." But he felt rattled, and when Maggie brought Coldgrave a glass of gin on ice, he began to blink nervously.

"All right," said Coldgrave, "I think we can get started, everyone. Bob, and of course George, have come to see us at Thanksgiving. Isn't that nice? And it's all so seasonal and cheery, isn't it? So, Bob, why don't you just go ahead and give us your little talk."

Maggie cleared her throat. "It's Christmas, Mary."

Coldgrave lowered her glass. "Yes, of course. Thank you, Maggie. Happy Christmas, then, everyone."

Sitting forward a little, Willard looked at them, then said, "I should just get to it, I suppose. I'm afraid there simply—isn't—the—"

But Gretchin cut in with, "They said no, right?"

He nodded. "Yes, I'm afraid that's correct. They said the funding just isn't there."

"Which is total bullshit."

"Now, Gretchin," he came back quickly, shifting a leg, "I wouldn't be hasty. Management has to prioritize, you know, it's a fact of life."

"Yeah, more bullshit. They're telling us that the only way to give us another driver is by having one of us get killed. God, that's cheap. Hey, Bradley, think of it, the Agency brass is cheaper than you are."

Willard stared at her helplessly, then simply looked at the floor.

Coldgrave, lowering her glass, offered, "Bob, is there something from our side that we could do? It seems quite unreasonable to have Bradley merely be driving all the time. He's a marvelous shot. And no one else here carries a .45, we need the stopping power. That bullet drops considerably at fifty yards, and is somewhat useless beyond a hundred, but at close range, well, hit a man with that and he's married his last girl."

His eyes went closed again. "I understand, Mary, I do, but they said no, and I can't go back to them."

Then Maggie said, "I may have a solution. As much as I hate to admit it, Lenny is bored, terribly bored. The range is interesting for him, and gun maintenance and other things are just right for him, but speaking as his wife, I know it just isn't enough. He needs to be back in the work."

Packard said nothing, but crossed his arms and smiled at her.

Willard looked at her, then at Packard. "How about it, Mr. Packard?"

The gunman shrugged. "What would I be doing exactly?"

"Driving. You'd be taking Osipov's place at the wheel. You're file said you're good with a car. And also, let's face it, the sheer firepower you sling about would be invaluable for the team, as it was before. Maggie, I won't say I hadn't thought of it, but I wasn't going to be the one to suggest it. He's your husband, you could lose him."

"At least," she returned, "he'd die content."

"Mary," said Willard, "what do you think?"

"That would solve everything," was the answer. "It would put Bradley back in the Corvette and in service with the .45, give us a driver for the SUV, add two .357's and a shotgun to our power, and obviously, put a goldmine of expertise in the field."

"So," he said, "Mr. Packard, it's up to you. The Agency would be paying you the same amount, you understand, I just can't alter that for now. But how about it?"

The rough fingers scratched the stubble. "Sounds good."

Willard brought his hands together with a pop. "Yes, then, very good, okay, it's solved, we have a resolution, people."

Gretchin squinted at him for this, and gave her head a shake.

Coldgrave held her glass aloft to catch Maggie's attention, then said, "You know, the .357 is a magnificent round. The trajectory is quite insignificant, and it hits about as hard at a hundred feet as right out of the muzzle. It is, in my opinion, the most versatile round in the security world."

"But you don't use it, Mary," said Willard, "I know this."

"True," she returned, "but I'm right up close and don't need the power. Neither do I need the muzzle rise with the lightweight. And who wants to lug the weapon mass necessary to tame the muzzle? With the 642, I do well with .38 P+, as does Kelly."

"Yeah," agreed Bobbie Lee, after a chug of beer, "even plus P's one goddamn hell of a whack in the head. Excuse my French."

Willard gave her a look of disapproval, then said, "Well, all right, then. Now let's move on to the next project I have for you. Again, I think you'll enjoy this one." He paused, hoping for a positive response, but seeing only that Gretchin was about to launch a protest, he hurriedly continued, "We have an entity, a semi-political group, one that we think consists of three men and two women, that is planning to carry out an attack on the U.S. embassy in Paris. We know it, because a disgruntled former sympathizer of the group called us to tell us they were going to do it. Normally we might just wait for them, but these people have left two corpses in their wake. One reason your team was chosen to stop them is because they're not bombers, they're gunmen, and they're good at it. You won't be encountering pushovers. They're amateurs certainly, but not pushovers, be warned. ... Now, these five people have been in West Virginia for about five months, living in a rented house and driving two rented cars—a GMC pickup truck and a Civic. They've committed countless petty infractions, as they have an apparently total disregard for the law. So, we could easily have them arrested, but of course, we don't want to do that. If it sounds simple, it isn't. Although we are certain that they are in the political group, we are not sure they constitute it, so we need their computers and phones. It's vital you search the house and cars and of course the bodies. Intel says they practice with their weapons at a local gun ranch nearly every day and for long hours. They are fairly stationary, as the house is in a rural area and they seem to stick pretty much close to home. They have the two cars, which is not good, and they take occasional walks in the woods around the house. Anyway, they are not always together, except at gun practice at the ranch. I would suggest you take two cars and the motorcycle."

"Oh," piped Bradley, "should we try out the Bentley?"

He grinned. "Probably not, Mr. Hopkins, probably not. Very funny though, I like that."

Coldgrave, who seemed not to get the joke, merely held out her glass, as if to consider whether she needed a refill.

"But, Mr. Packard," said Willard, "this would be a good situation for your rejoining the team, yes?"

Packard grunted an apathetic assent, then wiped his nose with an oil-stained thumb.

Coldgrave, after taking a sip from the glass, queried, "What is the time frame, Bob?"

"The house is rented by the month, so they could leave at any time. We want you to hit them within two weeks. So, Mary, please call me with a plan within, say, two days. Then, I would say, you should all pack up."

CHAPTER 22

West Virginia, January 2016

"Are you okay with this, Len?" queried Coldgrave, checking her lipstick in the mirror.

"With what?"

"Driving."

"Sure, it's just another tin box on wheels."

"Well, now, Mr. Packard, I meant driving for the team, doing that part of it *per se*. Still okay with that?"

"Sure. Don't worry, I'll be pulling a trigger or two."

She had to smile at his gruffness. Maggie had certainly found herself a wolf of a man to love. But he did seem to love her as much as she loved him. What a beautiful couple they made—she the refinement, he the grit, of the marriage. She looked out her window, then asked, "Why is it called an SUV?"

"It's for sport utility vehicle. You actually didn't know that?"

"No." And with a chuckle, "But that makes sense. And would you say we are out for the sport part or the utility part, Mr. Packard?"

"Both."

"Really?"

"Or take your pick. How the hell should I know?"

The gruffness again, so she smiled again. Reaching down, she withdrew the 642 from her purse, opened its cylinder, then closed it, then opened and closed it again. Holding the piece out flat in the palm of her gloved hand, she considered the perfection of its mechanism. And such a pretty gun, friendly, compact, a joy to handle and use. And who would want anything but smooth white bone for grips?

Observing this, he asked, "Where'd you learn so much about guns? Did they give you a course on it, or something?"

She dropped the gun into the purse. "No, it's a personal interest, that's all."

"Don't forget the pump's over the seat, full of triple-aught," and then, with a distinct grin that showed his yellow teeth, "just as a backup, of course, or in case you have to get through a door."

It was odd to have him engage in humor. She had never seen him actually laugh. Perhaps he saved this side of himself for Maggie, for their private moments, for their lovemaking. With a shiver, she turned her attention to the highway. "It does not seem cheerful here," she muttered. "Where are we?"

"Just crossed into West Virginia. You can tell by the bullet holes in the road signs. My kind of place.

They don't have a car accident down here, they wreck a car. Then they take it home and put it on display on cinder blocks in the front yard and to use for parts, and they take the seats out and put them on the porch for when company comes to visit. When they wreck another one, they drag the first to the backyard for their kids to use for target practice, then put the fresh wreck up on display on the cinder blocks."

"Is this more humor, Mr. Packard?"

"I hope not. I'm no damn joke teller, lady."

Momentarily, "Maggie's a wonderful person."

"She is. I love her to pieces."

"And do you like her?"

"I do, yes."

Bradley closed his eyes briefly.

"Getting tired?" queried Gretchin.

"Not a bit."

"You look tired."

"Nope, just glad to be back in the Vette."

"I think we should pull in somewhere for coffee."

"I'm full up, thanks."

"I saw your eyelids fall, Bradley."

"What, I can't blink? And what is it with watching me all the time?"

"Grow up," she said, "I'm not watching you. Think how sick that would make me."

"I'm saying, I'm not tired a bit."

"I think coffee would do us both good."

"I'm fine, ready to rock."

With a sigh, she looked out the windshield again. "Where are we?"

"West Virginia."

She opened her phone. "Nothing. I'm going to let them know we're in the state." She texted, *In wv now*, sent it to Coldgrave and Connors, and closed the phone. "Did you hear what the president did the other day? God, these people."

"He's the president."

"Yeah, yeah, but the whole pyramid-structure thing is as ironic as you can get. Hell, the president's more expendable than we are."

"You're nuts. You do too much philosophy, you know that?"

"Look at it this way," she said, "if he doesn't get shot, he's there for eight years max, right? Well, there's Roosevelt, but who cares about him? Most of them, eight years max. But we're way down the list, and if we don't get shot, we're here for twenty years or even more."

"Your point?"

"Willard, asshole that he is, said everybody in this business is expendable." She looked over at him again. "You don't remember, do you?"

"Sure, so what?"

"Think about it," she replied, "the lower down you go on the pole, the less expendable you are, I just showed you that. A secretary, for instance, even in the Agency, is going to be there until she pees her chair."

"Your point?"

"The general perception is that it's the other way around, stupid."

"And thinking, like this, helps you?"

Momentarily, "Look for a place, I want some coffee."

Bobbie Lee took a peek through the window at the Harley, then slid into the booth. She looked into the colorless eyes. "Okay, so far?"

"Sher. Me lag haerts, but I'm okay. T'anks for droivin'."

"Not a problem, girl."

"Where are we?"

"Wist Virginia. I would prefer Tinnessee, but it gits cold there too, I have to admit." Her eyes moved over the blond hair. "Why not come down to Tinnessee with me sometime?"

"I told you, et's too fuckin' hot."

"We could go in winter."

"Not on the boike."

"We could git a car, then. Come on, you'd jist love it. You can shoot your gun out in your yard there. Come on."

"You keep sayin' that, but I'm not sher I believe et."

"Trust me, it's true. Maybe not in the city, but we wouldn't be in the city. There's nothin' to see in the cities, except for Nashville and Mimphis, and yeah, I guess there's a lot there. We'd have a great time. I'm promisin', if you go to Tinnessee with me, I'll go to Irelan' with you. I'll show you the old Confid'racy, and you can show me all that IRA stuff. What say?"

"You'll prob'ly have me wearin' gray."

Bobbie Lee waved a hand. "Nah, you won't have to join my army, and I won't join yours neither. I wouldn't be in the IRA anyway, they're nuts."

"So's the Confad'racy."

"So, how 'bout it? I promise we'll git a car with a good heater, I guarantee it."

Connors looked at her. "Why not?"

Giving the table a tap, "All right, miss clover leaf, that's a date, we'll do it." Then looking around, "Hey, what say we git some more of them Frinch fries?"

The next morning, Gretchin rolled over and blinked at the sunlight filtering through the shabby curtain. In the next bed Bobbie Lee and Connors were still asleep. After going to the bathroom, she put her robe and slippers on and then stood on the cracked concrete just outside the door. Although she did not know it, before her, like a piece of mottled shag carpet, lay just a fragment of the Great Appalachian Valley.

Shivering, she pulled the robe up tighter around her neck. Across from the rooms, on the sloped lot, rested the Corvette, the SUV, and the Harley. Why did it feel like she didn't belong here? It was a pretty day. Unlike the cold of yesterday, this morning's chill, although threatening to drive her back inside, seemed cheery, almost poetic. But still, they had not come here on vacation, but on business.

Inside she showered and brushed her teeth. Bobbie Lee and Connors, after waking from their heavy sleep, did the same.

"We're all meeting at the diner we saw coming in," she announced, closing her phone. "About fifteen minutes, Mary said." Then she went outside and called Bradley.

As Connors came from the bathroom, Bobbie Lee said, "You ever think of gittin' plastic surgery for them scars?"

"What for, to be pretty?"

A shrug. "No, I'd say you're pritty enough, girl. Hell, you're like a movie star. You could go to Nashville right now."

"Then why?"

"I don't know, jist to cover up them scars."

"Why?"

"I don't know. It's like you're a beautiful sculpture, but a little restoration wouldn't hurt."

Connors smirked, "You mean I'm lookin' old?"

"No, classical. But you've been all shot up, girl."

"So've you."

"Not as much as you, you're like Swiss cheese, only prittier."

"Who cares?"

"I do," said Bobbie Lee. "But then, I think I like you jist the way you are. . . . Okay, no surgery."

Not far from the motel the little country restaurant and bar lay hidden by trees and a crumbling, bowed wall that had once been the side of a dog food factory. Its two chimneys smoking, the establishment peeked out at the highway as if uncertain whether to invite people to come in. After being offered a long table at the center of the dining area, Coldgrave requested a circular table in a corner.

"Did you sleep well, Mary?" queried Gretchin as the waiter brought menus.

"I did," replied Coldgrave, for she had booked a separate room, to give her privacy so she might collect her thoughts, as she said. "And you, Gretchin, I trust you slept well, and everyone else, yes? Another quaint place, isn't this? Where are we, Mr. Packard? I know we are in West Virginia, which is practically Timbuktu, but I mean, what part of the country, would you say?"

He looked at her. "We're in Appalachia, Mary."

"I've heard of that."

Bradley lowered his menu. "It's a long way from Fifth Avenue."

"Yes," she returned cheerily, "nothing posh, I can tell."

"Yeah, Mary," said Bobbie Lee, "if you can live here, you can live in Tinnessee."

The waiter was disappointed that no one wanted the early breakfast special, but amiably he took the orders anyway, apologizing to Coldgrave for the limited selection of alcohol. He could give her some Jack Daniel's or Wild Turkey over ice, but no mixed drink, he said, since the bartender wouldn't be arriving until mid-afternoon.

CHAPTER 23

Since the house stood on open ground, and visibility from its numerous windows and front porch was fairly unobstructed, surveillance beyond that already accomplished by intel was deemed unnecessary. The few passes made by the team along the macadam road during the late morning and early afternoon showed that both of the targets' vehicles had been utilized that day. It also showed that although the building seemed fairly defensible from a weapons standpoint, it was clearly vulnerable to onslaught by fire. Connor's suggestion, however, that the rickety two-story frame structure be surrounded in the early morning hours, set on fire, and its occupants shot upon exit, was rejected on fear that a standoff situation might ensue, or that the countryside might be set ablaze, or both. Besides, the computers would be lost.

That evening, after supper had been taken at the diner and a bottle of gin for Coldgrave had been procured from its bartender, when the team gathered for evening beer and chips in Coldgrave's room, other possible plans were forwarded.

"First off," said Gretchin, reaching for a chip, "if we hit them at the gun range, everybody there will simply think we're terrorists of some sort and turn on us. Personally, I'd rather do Kelly's house fire than go that route. I'm sure that down here everybody suspects every unfamiliar person of being a terrorist. So, I wouldn't want to screw with the locals, I'm sure they're all pretty much weapons proficient."

Bobbie Lee gave her nose a swipe. "You saying' all southerners are paranoid and trigger happy?"

Gretchin cleared her throat. "Well, let's say righteously paranoid, or whatever term you want me to use. But I wouldn't fuck with the people around here, judging from the bullet holes in the street signs, okay? What the hell's the difference, hitting these people at a gun range would be too goddamn dangerous, with everybody standing around with active weapons."

"Yeah, I agree," said Bradley. "The range thing would be a bad idea. We don't need to risk getting into a shooting war with the local militia."

Coldgrave set her glass down. "Mr. Packard, any ideas?"

A craggy grin. "At the range would be stupid. At the house would be risky, whether we shoot them out or burn them out. In either case, they would have time to call somebody. The best place to hit them would be on that macadam road that runs by the house. But how to get all five of them into the same car, I have no idea. We can't get close enough to the house to keep an eye on things, there's just too much open area. There is a curve in the road, with trees to hide maybe the motorcycle behind them. It's on the way from the house to the range. But it would be pot luck timing."

Coldgrave put the iced gin to her nose and inhaled the vapors thoughtfully. "The report from intel says they leave for the range every morning between nine and noon. Let's just try for a couple of days to catch them on the road. Otherwise, I'm afraid we're going to have to hit them in the morning at the house before they're awake, and count on casualties. . . . No, I don't want to go into that house."

"So," said Gretchin, "do you want us out on that road at about eight forty-five?"

"Perfect. Bobbie Lee, see if you two can find a spot off-road somewhere after that curve. And no texting, please, everyone, just call."

Draining her glass, Gretchin said, "I have one more thing to say, and I want everybody to think about it. The whole thing about minimal electronics for the team, I think, has got to go. Obviously we don't have to talk about it now, but it's the first thing I'm bringing up the next time Willard sticks his nose in the door. A simple examination on Google Earth would help us immensely, and these shitty flip phones, really? My point, we can upgrade without losing the creativity Paul talked about. The team was experimental then, it's not experimental anymore."

Coldgrave also put her glass down. "You want us to use smartphones?"

"Of course. That's all I use personally, just like you do, but I want to use it in the work. It makes sense, and it would make things a lot safer. I'm just giving everybody a heads-up that when we get back I'm bringing it up again to Bob."

When everyone had left, Coldgrave picked up the phone and called the desk. "Yes, hello, this is Mary Coldgrave. . . . Correct. . . . Well, I'm glad he did. Mr. Willard is a dear. . . . Yes, I would. Would you have any more of the clear ice, by chance? . . . Oh, many thanks. . . . That would be wonderful. . . . All right, see you then. Goodbye."

Twenty minutes later, a freshened drink beside her, she opened her phone to call Willard, but then shut it. She reached for the glass, imagining what could go wrong the next day. But he had known all along the precariousness of the project, what could be more obvious? And what could be more probable than that there should be casualties?

Bobbie Lee, throttling back, brought the Sportster's speed to ten, her eyes on the trees to her right. She was comfortable, thanks to the upgraded winter gear, but knew she could only speak for herself. Then, with the mighty engine at a bare chug, she headed off the blacktop and into the broken brush. Swinging the bike around, its tires crushing sticks, she put both boots down.

Pushing her visor up, she said over her shoulder, "It's idlin' real nice, right?"

Connors merely rested a confirming hand on the other's shoulder and swung off. "This esn't too bad," she said, wringing her gloved hands. "But ef I gat cold, I'm buildin' a foire."

"I don't think you're gonna git the chance, girl. I've got a feelin' 'bout this, and I'll betcha those creeps are headin' out right about now. See, it's a pritty day—why not git an early start at the range, that's what they'll be sayin'. And that's why I'm not shuttin' off. Besides it'll keep us warm." Here she gave the throttle a little twist.

Connors took a few steps toward the road, then returned. "You're roight, et's warmer here." Then she pulled up the top of the right saddle case, lifted the Glock, let it drop back into place, and gave a lift to each of the spare magazines.

Bobbie Lee grinned with admiration. "I love that new 26 you got there. And them fifteens you got stuck up its ass—boy, that's sexy! Can't wait to try it out mysilf. Fuckin' machine gun, nearly."

Closing the lid, Connors reached into her jacket pocket for the .38.

"Jist keep them shootin' gloves on, girl," Bobbie Lee continued, "or your hands'll freeze up if I have to rev it up some. And if I was you, I'd skip the .38 and go for the Glock, or you'll git yoursilf shot right off the back of this here rocket ship. They said these fuckers go to the range, so they've got their hands on their guns right now in them cars." And reaching into the front of her own jacket, she felt for the magnum.

Then Connors' phone rang out from her jacket. "Yeah? . . . Roight. . . . Two? Yous take the truck, we'll take the lettle one. . . . Bye."

"Oh boy, what's up, girl?"

With a fiendish grin, "They're out and headed for the range. We're takin' the lettle one. Lat's go." Then she swung her leg over and found the pegs.

Bobbie Lee booted back the kickstand and shifted into first. "Hell shit, I hear somebody comin' now."

As the bike began to roll, Connors flexed her fingers inside the soft gloves. Even now she could see the pickup as it rounded the curve. It was followed by the Civic, and farther back, the SUV.

When the three vehicles had passed, Bobbie Lee throttled up and sent the Harley roaring out onto the blacktop. She soon pulled them up behind the SUV and watched for a signal from Coldgrave. She was relieved when Connors flipped the hard bag's lid and pulled up the 26.

"All right, Gretchin, very nice," said Coldgrave into her phone. "You'll see us soon. The truck's out in front—a man and a woman. Then the Civic—two men and a woman. . . . I'm sending Kelly after the Civic now, then we'll pass them and go after the truck. . . . Right, that's right. We may be coming at you at high speed. Be careful. Take care. . . . Right. . . . Okay, here we go. . . . Bye." And closing the phone, she said to Packard, "Wait for Kelly to start, then pass them and bring us up to the truck." Then she turned and through the rear window caught Bobbie Lee's attention and waved her forward.

Bobbie Lee, at this signal, moved into the oncoming lane, quickly accelerated past the SUV to bring them up beside the Civic. Instantly Connors stuck the Glock out and began firing into the left rear window at the driver's back—*Bam! Bam! Bam! Bam! Bam! Bam!* But suddenly a handgun was shoved out the blown-in rear window by a woman in the backseat and was fired twice—

Pop! Pop! Instantly Connors returned fire—*Bam! Bam! Bam! Bam!*

Bobbie Lee kept the Harley close to the Civic, but as the SUV now blew past to attack the truck, the little car began to slow and move into the bike, sideswiping it. Already Connors was firing in at the second man in front—*Bam! Bam! Bam! Bam! Bam!* Bobbie Lee, increasing speed and moving away from the moribund car, watched as Coldgrave, magnum out the window, fired into the side of the truck.

As Bobbie Lee heard the Civic crash into the trees back to her left and felt Connors shoving home another fifteen mag, she watched as the truck ahead was suddenly wrenched left to ram the SUV. She throttled up more, but then backed off, for Coldgrave now had leveled Packard's second magnum and was emptying it into the truck's door again. The passenger, a woman, had grabbed the steering wheel to stabilize the vehicle and seemed to be trying to reach the brake to stop it. But the SUV's door opened and Coldgrave stood up and with her .38 fired three shots at the woman.

As the SUV and motorcycle now slowed the truck veered suddenly right, ran through the thick brush and boom-crashed into the trees. The Corvette, approaching from the opposite direction pulled up to the crash site and stopped. The SUV did the same.

But making a U-turn, Bobbie Lee headed the Harley back toward the first crash site. Reaching it, she swung the bike around, pulled to a stop, and let the engine idle.

"Did she hit you?" she queried.

Connors swung off. "Not sher. Somethin' het me jacket. Here's a hole, maybe I've got a hole en me tet."

"Unzip it, girl, right now."

Connors obeyed, but found nothing but an exit hole in the other side of the jacket front. Then she turned and trudged through the brush to the car, where methodically she put two shots into the head of each occupant.

Bobbie Lee watched as Connors then removed her shooting gloves and pulled on rubber gloves from her pocket. Minutes later she returned, carrying a plastic bag with three bloody phones and two rubber gloves in it. By the time they reached the second site, Coldgrave had already done the same to the truck's occupants, and Bradley was bagging their phones.

Stepping up to the Harley as it rolled to a stop, Coldgrave said, "They're coming with us to search the house. Don't think we'll need you."

"Roight," replied Connors, handing her the bag.

"Good," said Coldgrave, "glad you used rubber gloves this time."

Then Bobbie Lee pulled her visor down, sent the big machine into a U-turn, and throttled up.

CHAPTER 24

The Estate

Nearly in unison Willard and George smiled, then sipped their tea.

"Ah," remarked the former, smacking his lips, "it is certainly lovely here, isn't it, George?" And not waiting for a response, "Maggie, could I just have another of those chocolate chips? They're out of this world, as usual."

"Certainly," replied Maggie sweetly, drawing the cart closer.

He smiled at her again, following her with his eyes as she performed this familiar routine. He loved it when the pieces fell into place like this. Taking a bite from the cookie, he closed his eyes and munched contentedly. Then he heard Gretchin's voice.

"Bob," she said, her tone missing the sweetness of Maggie's, "I want to bring up the electronics issue again. I can see a couple of the points to Kessler's approach, but some I cannot. I'm sure they had some bearing at one time, but now, I don't know."

Wondering why she couldn't have waited at least until he had swallowed his heavenly mouthful of cookie, he replied, "Sure, Gretchin, what specifically do you mean?"

"The cell phones. I mean, there are phones out there that'll really cook, and these flip phones are slow as hell. That slowness could result in a casualty."

"But we've already talked that out," he said meekly. "We don't want the team to use smartphones in the work, as I've explained to you. You can have one and use it as much as you want, of course, just not in the work. And you know the reasons already."

Her tone flaring, "What do you mean, *you can have one,* what the hell is that? You don't tell me I can have one, I've got one, fucker. Don't talk down to me, I hate that, just respond to my goddamn logic, if you don't mind."

Slowly, as if forcing himself to speak after a shock, he said, "All right, I understand. You don't need to get heated over it."

Calmly she continued, "With a smartphone, we can text each other simply by voice."

He shook his head. "They're slower, not faster, believe it or not. We've done tests ourselves. Gretchin, I have a smartphone and use the voice feature on it. It can be very helpful. But the tests, at least the Agency's tests, show that if you practice texting with buttons, you can actually do it faster. It's because both touch screens and voice features are so problematic in imperfect conditions, which seem innumerable. Voice can't be used on a motorcycle, for instance, except with a microphone, and a touch screen is useless in the rain or if it's too cold out. But besides that," and holding up a forefinger, "this team, which has been funded generously, I have to say, was meant to be unique. Part of that uniqueness is creativity, as you know, and the Agency, at this point, believes that can be best fostered by maintaining the paradigm. Obviously as a team you are still experimental. Eventually the Agency intends to use the model to form other teams for the same type of work. So, we want the team to stay the same, as much as possible."

"God, that was a mouthful. So, how about GPS?"

"Absolutely not."

"But you give us time frames, vitally important time frames, which we might very well miss just stumbling around looking for some silly street."

He gave her a condescending smile. "Well, the team has done all right so far. Maybe we shouldn't try to fix it, huh?"

Then her eyes began to glow again. "You're talking down to me. Don't do it."

His expression sobered. "I didn't mean to, Gretchin. Sorry."

But she turned to Maggie and muttered, "The condescending asshole."

"Bob," put in Coldgrave, "isn't there a compromise you could offer?"

Blinking, he said, "No, there isn't, Mary. It's not up to me, and I've been instructed to keep things the way they are. You can upgrade, of course—new guns, regular equipment, things like that, but still no automatic weapons, explosives or poisons."

"The same as before," said Maggie. "I think we can manage to remember most of it, Bob."

He must not allow sarcasm to pass for genuine discontentment, so he looked away from her to Gretchin and said, "I understand that there are a few things you find unbearable about working with the team, Gretchin. But there are also many amenities you must enjoy. There's the pool, for instance, think of how you enjoy swimming, and there's lots of time for vacation."

Giving him a hard look, she went to the cart and got herself another lager from the ice bucket.

He brought his foot to his knee. "Does anyone else have a comment?" Momentarily, he continued, "Well, then, I have to say, the team's work on this last project was remarkable. I'm surprised none of you was hurt. You're still very lucky, you know. But efficiency—well! Five body bags and two rental cars, not bad. Two of the phones weren't secure and have proven useful. The desktop from the house is being examined. Quite a haul, thanks very much. And I'm pleased that it worked out for you, Mr. Packard. Welcome back." After taking another sip of his tea, he said, "So, everybody, I think that's about it. . . . Oh yes, and I think a vacation for everyone is in order."

Giving him another hard look, Gretchin returned, "My soul isn't for sale, Bob, thanks. My body is, but not my soul."

"You know, sir," said George, turning onto the highway, "that Ms. Wheeler is really insolent. Are you sure you want to put up with that?"

"Yes, she is, George, I understand that. Insolent and profane, quite profane. And listening to her puts a pain in my stomach, I can assure you. But you have to consider the source, George. She was just a public school teacher, and an art teacher at that. I don't know about you, but in my experience artists are pretty much vile by nature. So, from a source like that, well, I have to cut her some slack."

"But she is intelligent, sir, she understands, it seems to me, just when she's crossing a line. And she crosses it all the time."

"I agree, she is intelligent, but she is also an artist, and that means she's intelligent with a screw loose—not a good combination."

"I understand, sir. But she has a heart, and it seems to me that she's directing a lot of animosity, maybe even hatred, in your direction."

"A heart, George, really? I'm not sure she's got much of a human heart. Oh, she's got a heart, sure, but more like the heart of a reptile, a snake, a dragon."

"And that's not good, sir?"

Willard looked away and out the window. "No, George, it isn't."

"So," said Maggie, switching off the lamp on her nightstand, "you made it through. Well, of course, I'm glad."

Packard, his eyes closed, responded with a mere grunt.

"Was it very dangerous?"

"I don't know. There was lead in the air."

"But you're happy, right?"

"I'm happy that it's important to you that I'm happy."

She gave him a tap under the covers. "Don't get philosophical on me. The point is, you are happier in the field than out of it, correct?"

"I guess."

"And riding with Mary, any problems there?"

"Why should there be?"

"Just asking, dear."

"No problems," he murmured, "she's a great girl."

"Is she as good as Gretchin says?"

"Better."

"Gracious."

"She could hold her own with Connors, I think. They're both scary, real pros. They've got what I've got. It's great to work with them."

"And the others?"

"Why're you asking? You know as well as I do."

"I'm just talking, Lenny. I think I simply want to hear your voice. If things had gone wrong on the project, I might not be heaaring your voice right now, so indulge me."

"Okay. Bobbie Lee has it, too, and Gretchin's getting there. Bradley does not have it. He's good with a gun, but not with death. I doubt he'll ever have it. Some people just have a block."

"I'm sorry, dear."

"But Connors and Mary, that's nuclear."

"Which makes them very valuable to the Agency."

"Of course," he replied. And with a chuckle, "But I wouldn't sell them any life insurance."

She gave his stubbled chin a tweak. "Well, I'd sell you some, dear, because you've got me to come home to."

"Yeah, and because you'd make money if I didn't come home."

"Didn't mean it that way."

A low soft growl, like the sigh of a wolf. "I know."

Gretchin opened the door and looked at him inquisitively.

"Hey," he said, "how's it going?"

"What do you want, Bradley?"

"Just to talk."

"It's late, did your aviator watch stop?"

"I was wondering, would you like to go out for dinner and a movie, say, tomorrow night?"

She looked at him, giving herself a moment. "Sure. What time?"

"I don't know," he replied, with a shrug.

"Well, come up with something."

"Yeah, okay. How about we leave at five?"

"Okay, see you then." And without waiting for his response, she closed the door. But she did listen for his steps as he walked away. Then she sat on the bed again and took up her smartphone. Touching the app icon, she moved through the list. Then she looked toward the door again, recalling how he had come to her that first time years before. They'd been together many times, but now it was different, almost distasteful. She liked men, she loved men, loved their look, their smell, the sound of their voice, but then, she hated them, too. Why was life like that? Why did it have to find you, grab you, control you? And why did it have to screw you over every single goddamn time it got its hands on you? Why couldn't it just let you alone to enjoy being alive? Why did it have to trip you up, knock you up, beat you up?

Then she put the phone down and went to the closet. What should she wear tomorrow night? Did it matter?

At three minutes before five, Bradley knocked on the door, expecting a significant wait. But it opened immediately and he looked at her.

"Hi," she said.

His eyes moved over the hair. He had always liked red hair, or maybe not, he couldn't remember. And he had always liked green eyes. "Hi," he said, "I'm sorry I'm early, I had wanted to give you time to get ready."

Glancing back at the clock, "That would be two minutes?"

"So," he said, "are you ready, or do you need more time?"

"Jesus!" she breathed, with a shake of her head. And pulling the door closed, "Let's just go."

If the ride to Philadelphia had traditionally been problematic for them, this evening it wasn't. They did not argue about anything, and the bleak winter countryside seemed pleasant.

"Warm enough?" he queried, accelerating onto 76 east.

"Perfect," she replied. "Put some music on."

"Sure, what?"

"Anything."

He flipped down the CD rack. "Uh, how about country?"

She shivered. "How about not? Do you have any jazz?"

Turning on the radio, he replied, "Sure. It's a Philly station. Here you go."

"No CD's?"

"No, sorry."

After dinner, when they were walking through the frosty air, she took his arm. She could not smell him, but she knew his smell, so it didn't matter. The city sounds, smells, lights, the myriad of people, all seemed charming. Life wasn't always bad, to be sure. But it did seem always to have bad intentions.

"What movie would you like to see?" he asked as they approached the Ritz. "I don't even know what's out. We could see an action movie for me, or a chick flick for you."

Her eyes went closed. "Something in between maybe?"

"And I'm going to get coffee and a candy bar. How about you?"

She remembered later, after the movie, when they were having tea in a cafe, that she had not answered him. But now she wanted him to ask it again. She watched as his eyes went down the menu of teas on the wall above their table.

"I'm getting a piece of pie," he said, "and English breakfast tea, like Maggie's."

She waited, but he said nothing, so she said, "I'll have the same."

When he had gotten the things at the counter and placed them on the table, she saw that he would not look at her. Then she saw that he was looking down at his pie, as if unable to look up.

"Something wrong?" she queried.

Then he did look up. "Would you marry me?"

She closed her eyes for a moment, then opened them. "Yes, Bradley, I will."

And as he continued to look at her she could see his surprise at the tears in her eyes.

CHAPTER 25

In April, on a fresh day, under a brightly painted blue sky, standing poolside in the shade of the umbrellas of three tables brought together to form an enclosure, Gretchin Wheeler and Bradley Hopkins were married, with Margaret Swift-Jones Packard as best woman and Leonard Packard as best man. Stanislav Osipov performed the ceremony. The great Tai Ping and the mighty German Shepherd Helga were ring bearers. Kelly Connors and Bobbie Lee Henry, both visibly armed, stood to the side as guardians for the proceedings. Afterward, Mary Coldgrave, as mistress of ceremonies, announced the married couple at the reception.

For security reasons, the group attending was kept small. Willard and George, of course, were there. They had stood awkward during the whole ceremony, as if forced to be there. At times, Willard could not but scowl at the presence of Osipov, who had come from Moscow at the invitation of none other than Coldgrave herself. Turning away at one point, he muttered to George that it had probably not been necessary for her to pay his travel expenses, since he had made out like a bandit following his wife's death.

"I've not seen a wedding gown in black before, sir," remarked George during the poolside reception.

The other lifted an eyebrow. "Neither have I, George," he said. "Looks especially weird, don't you think, with that green dragon crawling down her neck? Tattoos are gross. Remind me never to do that to myself, George. And look at her hair—like a fire."

George tipped up his beer and let it chug.

"I didn't know you drank," said Willard.

"Only occasionally, sir. I'll just have this one."

"Please, yes. Or I'll have to drive back, right?"

Maggie's opinion that catering would be necessary even for such a limited number of people proved wise. Neither she nor Bobbie Lee had cherished the responsibility anyway. Although the catering company had been approved by Agency security, none of its personnel were permitted at the ceremony or reception. Thus, Maggie and Bobbie Lee had agreed to at least tend the food and refreshment table, while Connors had agreed to keep the coffee coming.

Photography was provided by Osipov, who had brought his new video and photography equipment. For the ceremony, he had simply let the video run, while activating a still-shot camera remotely, but after the bride had been kissed, he repositioned the video camera to the end of the pool and slung the still-shot to wield himself. When

Gretchin reminded him that years before she had tried to get him to take nudes of her, and reminisced how she had awkwardly called with the proposal during his dinner date with Martina, he said he had not forgotten. Bradley, making the reception rounds with her, turned red upon hearing it.

Afterward, when everyone had eaten and drunk and taken a share both in reminiscing and in predicting the future, Packard brought the Corvette from the stable, and the newlyweds got in and drove away. They waved through open windows, but only Gretchin actually looked back. Spotting Maggie waving from the doorway of the Big House, she started to cry, but then quickly announced that she was determined to be happy with turning this corner in her life. Bradley did not reply, but simply moved the windows up and turned the air conditioner on.

"You washed the car," she said after they had reached the interstate.

"Of course," he replied proudly. "You always appreciate a clean car, so I did it for you."

Momentarily, "But you wouldn't have done it for yourself?"

"Nah, it was okay. You like things clean though, so, yeah."

"You mean, you actually wouldn't have washed the car even for your own wedding? I mean, you're always washing your precious car, but you wouldn't have washed it for your own wedding?"

He swallowed. "Well, I would have, if it had been dirty, but it wasn't. I just did it for you—because I know how critical you can be."

She looked over at him. "Critical?" she repeated. "You know how critical I can be? Jesus. What, in God's name, have I done?"

"Well," he replied meekly, "you've married me."

She looked out the windshield to the highway, then out her window to the fields. "Yes," she said, "I have married you. . . . And you do look nice in your black suit." Then, after a moment, "You're supposed to respond by complimenting me on my dress."

Nearly stuttering, "Yes, it looks really great. It makes you look, like, twenty-five."

She looked at him again, as if to burn him with rays from her eyes. "I'm sixty-one, and you fucking well know it."

"I know," he replied even more meekly, "but in that dress you don't at all look your age."

"Jesus!" she uttered. "Just don't talk anymore, okay?"

He held up a pleading hand. "I'm not talking. You always talk a lot, I'm just listening. So, what did I do wrong?"

Her eyes went shut. "Nothing, Bradley. Just drive the fucking car, please."

Then she thought of how it might be in Bermuda, how he might be more sensitive and she less critical. How together they could swim and walk and have dinners and look at sunsets. How they could make love and talk of their future. But life wasn't like that, she considered, it never actually fulfilled wishes or let dreams come true. It changed reality into fantasy just when you were most vulnerable, and then, just as you believed and were beginning to trust the whole goddamn thing to be true, it pulled a whammy and changed everything back again, leaving you with a tricked heart and a tricked soul. Then she heard herself asking him if he thought they might be happy in Bermuda, and she heard him answer that it was always possible.

In May, after Gretchin and Bradley had returned from their honeymoon, Willard came again, to present a new project. He suspected, after inspecting them for the rosier cheeks that returning honeymooners were supposed to have, but finding only tans, that things had not gone so well. But he was hopeful that, since the couple did seem to be more relaxed with each other, the regularity of their sleeping arrangement would help her to be a little less volatile.

"It's amazing," he said to Packard poolside, watching as the newlyweds, walked hand-in-hand, toward them from the house, "how a simple good night's sleep can help one to be more positive about life."

"What the hell's that supposed to mean?" was the growled reply.

"Nothing, Mr. Packard, forget it."

After the rest of the team arrived and had spread their blankets and chosen their tables, Coldgrave cleared her throat and spoke. "We welcome Bob and George back again today, of course, and expect to have a profitable briefing, or discussion, or whatever you want to call it. Anyway—Bob?"

Willard smiled at this and brought his hands together, as if to collect his thoughts. "Thank you, Mary," he said. "First off, I do want to congratulate our newlyweds upon their return from Bermuda. Mr. and Mrs. Hopkins, congratulations again on your marriage, and welcome back."

After making a click with her tongue, Gretchin said, "We live here, and you're welcoming us back?"

He looked at her. "Well, I just mean it's good to have you back. Did you guys enjoy Bermuda?"

"We did," answered Bradley. "Nice place. Not sure I'd want to pay the rent to live there, but it was great."

Willard cocked his head. "Did you ride the little motorbikes?"

"Yeah, it was all great, thanks."

Squinting at the reply, Willard then said, "Okay—new project. There are malignant entities out there right now who want to disrupt anything and everything associated with the U.S. Government. One of those entities is an individual who hates—"

He was stopped by the hulky presence of Tai Ping, who had ambled between his chair and George's chair, on his way to the other side of the pool, where his water dish was stationed. Waiting for the fearsome dog to pass, he nearly held his breath. In fact, everyone watched the dog, his rolling muscles, his massive head, his fiery eyes, following him with their eyes until he had reached the dish.

"Incidentally," he said, "has that dog, uh, Mr. Tai, ever—"

Again he was cut off as Gretchin snapped, "Don't call him that. It's Tai Ping, just Ping, or even Mr. Ping, or even Tai, if you have to, but never Mr. Tai, don't call him that."

"Okay," he said, blinking. "But has he ever, uh, bitten, you know, hurt, anybody?"

"No," answered Bobbie Lee, "he's killed things, lots of things, but no people yit, at least not here."

"Sure, I understand. But I was thinking, if he bites somebody, there could be a problem with insurance."

"Oh," she replied, reaching for her beer, "we don't worry about that around here."

He looked at her. "All right, um, let's go on, then. Where was I?"

"You were telling us," said Coldgrave, "about an individual who hates."

"Oh yes, right. Well, we have had a guy on our radar for a long time, someone whose hatred for our government has apparently gotten the best of him. He has informed the Agency that he has decided to kill one of our agents. Do you believe it? *We* do. Story short—he has communicated with us the names of ten of our people working in China. Who knows where he got the information, but the list is correct, and there you have it. We do not wish to pull any of the agents, even if we knew which one he will target, as it is important to maintain all of them where they are. Further, after selecting his person and having them eliminated, he intends to inform the Chinese of the others. Given the importance of their placement, we would normally just inform them of the threat. But we've gotten a break. We know who and where this man is."

Suddenly Gretchin set her beer down and said, "I would like to propose another change."

"Not now," he groaned. "I would like to finish, if I may."

"I propose," she continued, "that Stanley be rehired for the team, both as a driver and as a surveillance person."

"That's impossible. I told you before, Gretchin, the Agency said he had to go, since he had been allowed to come on board only to get Martina back. I was very clear about it."

"We need him."

He gave her a hard look. "I don't care if you do."

"Ask Mary, go ahead. We need him for surveillance especially, and he's a photographer, he'd be perfect."

Willard closed his mouth and dropped his gaze. Then asked, "Mary, what about this?"

Coldgrave, lowering the glass from under her nose, replied, "I think he would be a great asset, and Gretchin's right, we do need somebody for surveillance. I agree, Osipov would be perfect."

"Well, that's ridiculous," he said, his tone desperate. "He was an infiltrator, for goodness' sake. That's a spy. You don't get that?"

Gretchin, stuffing hair behind an ear and reaching for her beer, returned, "No, we don't get that, Bob. The Agency practically killed his wife and then fired him, that's what we get."

He was incredulous, and his mouth fell open. "What?"

"You owe him, buster, big time. And we like him—a lot. We want him back." Then casually she tipped up the bottle and let it chug.

Willard, reddening, looked at George, then back at Gretchin. "Well, I can't do that. There's no money for it, for one thing. And for another, I don't trust him. He was a Russian spy. This team caught him, for goodness' sake." And glaring at her. "Your husband here never liked him, either—I mean, he never trusted him. Isn't that so, Bradley?"

Slowly and deliberately she turned her head and put her eyes upon her husband. "How about that, dear?"

Straightening himself, Bradley put his chin out, then replied, "Uh, I did think he might have been more positive about—well, you know, America and everything." And with her eyes upon him and his breathing rate increasing, he added, "But he was okay. He and I had great talks and stuff. So, I guess I can see the point that as a photographer he would be very good at surveillance."

She looked back to Willard. "See?"

With all his strength to control his rage, he looked once more to Coldgrave. "How did this happen? You're the team leader, Mary."

But Coldgrave merely put the glass to her nose again, leisurely breathed in the alcohol, then took a drink and let the liquid roll around in her mouth.

"Don't go picking on her," warned Gretchin hotly, "you just tend to your own goddamn business, mister. Talk about whose responsibility something was—Jesus! If there was anything we needed on the last project, it was surveillance. And it was you who sent us there, superman. What, were you trying to get us all killed like Martina?"

It was this that pushed him over the edge. "Stop it!" he barked. "Don't say things like that. I tell you what to do, you don't tell me what to do. Gracious, you are insolent!"

Lightly setting her beer on the table, she simply held forth her hand, then popped out the middle finger at him.

Briefly his mouth fell open, then he began to blink. Swallowing hard, he said, "I don't know what to say. My, uh, my impression was that the Osipov file was closed and that there shouldn't be any further discussion about it. But—well—I will take another look at the situation, if that's what everybody here wants. Would that satisfy everyone?"

Coldgrave set her glass down, as if about to speak.

But reaching out for the glass, Maggie queried, "Could I freshen that for you, Mary?"

"Oh yes, thank you, Maggie. That would be splendid."

"Nolet's?"

"Yes, that would be excellent."

"Anyone else?"

Bradley folded his arms. "Wow, Nolet's," he said, grinning broadly. "Know what that stuff costs?"

"Bradley," said Gretchin, "please."

"Well," he said, still grinning, "I couldn't drink it on my salary, I'll tell you that."

"My goodness," said Willard, clearly at the end of himself, "I think I'm losing my sanity just dealing with you people."

"But as I was going to say," said Coldgrave, looking at him, "that would satisfy us all, Bob. Yes, I think it would. And it's good of you to offer to look into it. I'm hopeful that something might be worked out. Having Stanley back with us would be helpful, even inspiring."

After considering the stupified expression on Willard's face, Gretchin said, "I have another point to bring up." And watching his eyes go closed at this, she said, "A housekeeper, someone to help Maggie with things, that would be helpful. The Agency turned down our other request, because of the lack of funding, of course. So, how about now? It's too much for Maggie. We want someone in at least once a week to do house cleaning—before the work kills Maggie, Martina's best friend."

He stared at her, then replied meekly, "Uh, uh, yes, I'll try to get that done."

"Soon," said Gretchin. "The work is killing her."

"And now," said Coldgrave, "why don't you continue, Bob, with telling us about the project?"

His expression was of simple shock as he looked from her to Gretchin. "Uh, yes," he murmured pathetically, "I guess that would be a good idea."

Maggie, setting the freshened drink at Coldgrave's place, asked sweetly, "Bob, where is this individual? You haven't told us that."

He put his hand on his brow, then said, "No. No, I haven't. He is in New Jersey, of all places,

Cherry Hill, New Jersey. He lives in a rented basement, which he has filled with computer equipment, of course. I don't want to identify the person who tipped us off about him, but well, just don't let anything happen to his landlady. Now, we have no idea how he plans to either kill or have someone kill one of our agents in China and no time to find out. We just want him neutralized as soon as possible. He could pull any number of tricks from his cyber world's bag. We cannot afford to wait, and the placement of our agents is far too sensitive to risk exposure." Here he reached for a briefcase and extracted from it three eight-by-tens. "Pass these around. Take a good look, he's a winner."

"Real geeky," said Bobbie Lee.

Chuckling, "I know. Love the glasses, right? That brings up another problem. This geek is so geeky he has the place under complete camera surveillance twenty-four seven. I don't know how you're going to get to him, let alone kill him. The landlady says he's extremely paranoid, suspicious of everyone and every situation. He could easily take her hostage. And if he did, he'd kill her. She's really sweet, so be careful not to get her hurt."

"That's great," said Gretchin. "The whole place is wired, he's fucking nuts, and you want us to protect her in what might turn into a horrific gunfight?"

"Well, that is precisely what you guys do, correct? Anyway, don't bother with collecting his computers, we'll get those."

"Phone?" asked Bradley.

"Yeah, get that, sure. But just ignore the rest, the cleanup crew will take care of it. Anyway, he's your dog, so go get him."

Now Bobbie Lee frowned. "I don't like jokes like that. I'm a shoot-the-man but save-the-dog kind of person."

"I thought you people weren't moralists," he returned, "except, of course, for Bradley."

"I'm not," she said. "But I do know what's valu'ble, and most times, the dog is and the man ain't."

He lifted his hands. "Okay, you've got me, I give up. In any case, there's no dog, so, just go get him. And remember, be careful to keep the landlady out of it."

Packard extracted a frayed handkerchief, blew his nose, then queried, "Is this guy alone? Any friends?"

A sigh. "Not sure, Mr. Packard. Intel just hasn't had a chance to spread him out. I'm sorry. We don't even know if he's armed. The landlady doesn't know, only says she thinks he's dangerous. The gun laws in New Jersey are pretty strict, but so what, right? Anyway, here's the rest of the packet. Not much info, I'm afraid."

Then he closed the briefcase, snapped it, and gripped its handle. Giving Gretchin and Coldgrave a chilly glance, he got up.

CHAPTER 26

Cherry Hill, New Jersey

"I don't want to go around again," said Coldgrave. "Everybody all right with that?" When there was no response, she said, looking at her phone, "Where's Audubon?"

"About five miles west," returned Gretchin from the back seat. "Audubon's nice, right, Bradley boy?"

"Don't call me that, please."

"Ah, he's sensitive."

"Good," said Coldgrave, "they should be here soon. Len, are you all right?"

A yawn. "Yep. Didn't get enough sleep. I could use a cold beer."

"You are not alone, sir." She looked at the phone again. "Actually they have just passed the house to take a look."

"Yeah," said Packard, adjusting his rearview mirror, "they're behind us."

"As if we couldn't tell," quipped Bradley. "They do make quieter bikes, you know. I think we should start a fund."

"All right," said Coldgrave, "everybody knows the plan. Here we go." Lifting the phone, she placed the call. "Hello, is this Mrs. Klein? ... Good. Mrs. Klein, I think you know who we are. We'll be there in a few minutes. Please try to answer the door when we ring. Does the bell work? ... Fine. See you in a few minutes. Please be ready. Oh, and, Mrs. Klein, don't be alarmed if we physically pull you out of the house, just do what we tell you, all right? ... No, don't run, don't do that, just do exactly what we say. ... That's fine, we'll see you shortly. ... Yes, bye." Then she texted Connors.

Packard moved the shift, and accelerated. Completing the turns around the block, he pulled to the curb. "This okay?" he queried.

But Coldgrave merely looked at him, then checked her mirror. Now Connors was at her window. Without her helmet, the blondness of her hair, set aglow by the sunlight, seemed especially intense, beautiful.

"We're ready," said Coldgrave, dropping the window. "No changes, all set."

Then she got out, and the two of them walked at a fast pace along the sidewalk. Turning at the walkway, they soon stepped to the slab at the front door and pressed the bell. Packard, watching them, heard Bobbie Lee goose the Harley, then in the mirror he saw her pull in the clutch. Then, even as Coldgrave slid her hand into her windbreaker and Connors reached up under her sweatshirt, the

213

inside door was pulled open and the storm door was pushed out.

First Coldgrave, then Connors, slipped through the opening.

"He's in the basement," said the woman as she stepped aside. Trembling, she added, "There, that door. He has a gun."

"Get out, walk to the curb," Coldgrave commanded the woman as Connors put her hand on the knob of the basement door.

Not waiting for the woman to leave, Connors turned the knob, pulled the door open, and went down the stairs, Coldgrave just behind her.

In two seconds she saw a man sitting at a desk, and yelled, "Turn around!"

But he only continued in the same position, staring with widened eyes at the guns of the two women. "What do you want?" he muttered.

"Looks loike hem to me," said Connors, instantly opening fire and pulling the trigger until the gun was empty.

"Ah-h!" he screamed as he sank in the huge chair, his hands gripping the armrests, his glasses falling to the floor.

But Coldgrave, already stepping over to him, now leveled her gun and fired into his hanging head—*Pop! Pop! Pop!*

Connors, who had reloaded and reholstered, now pulled on latex gloves and grabbed the bloodied pocket of the man's jeans. "Dump hem out," she said, unable to get into the tight pocket.

After Coldgrave had replaced her shooting gloves with latex gloves, the two women pulled the chair from the desk, then heaved it over, dumping the man. From the prone body Connors pulled the phone and bagged it, while Coldgrave pressed and held the computer's power button until the machine went off.

"Good t'ing we're usin' gloves," said Connors, "his blood's prob'ly full of shet."

Coldgrave gave a nod. "Look at all this filth, like mud on a rainy day. And there must be, what, ten computers down here?"

"Yeah, and camera surveillance round the clock, yat he missed us, dedn't he?"

Coldgrave pulled her gloves off and dropped them into the bag. "Let's go."

Bradley was standing beside the SUV, waiting for them. The woman, in the back seat and obviously traumatized, was being consoled by Gretchin. Packard, paying the woman no attention at all, seemed to be dozing. Behind the SUV, Bobbie Lee sat grinning on the Harley as it chugged at idle.

"I simply didn't know what to do," the woman blubbered. "I was scared to death when you called, and when you came to the door I just fell apart. I am so sorry."

"Well," returned Connors, pulling on her helmet, "you go down to that basemant of yours, and you'll be so scared you'll navver slape again."

Gretchin gave Connors a roll of the eyes. "Thank you for that, Kelly."

"Why?" queried the woman, her eyes widening. "What's down there?"

Fastening her chinstrap and turning toward the motorcycle, Connors merely replied, "A carpse, lady, with eight fuckin' holes en et. You moight want to wear rubber boots."

Coldgrave closed her phone, then said to the woman, "A crew will be here any minute to clean up. Would you like to join us for lunch somewhere?"

The answer was yes, but the voice was drowned by the blatting from the Harley's pipes as it tore away.

The Estate

"You mean," said Willard to Coldgrave as he and George sat for tea the next day, "that you simply went through the front door without considering another way to get in? And you just called the woman on the spot? What about her, what about keeping her safe, as I requested?"

Not waiting for Coldgrave to answer, Connors, extracting a beer from the ice bucket, said, "She's safe, corract?"

"But you put her at risk, when I asked you not to."

"She's foine, there's a carpse en a bag, and your agents are safe, so what the fuck do you care about resk?"

With a shake of his head, "Well, I'm shocked. I expect you all to do exactly as I say when the public is involved. I'm shocked, that's all."

"So," she returned, popping the cap off, "you won't be shocked next toime, you'll know what to expact."

"Oh, so, you're going to systematically ignore my instructions?"

She sat down. "No, but when they're shet, they're shet. Et's defferant en the field, try et sometoime. You try goin' ento a basemant and shootin' a fucker, then tell me how to do et."

"Kelly has a point, Bob," said Coldgrave. "It's visceral out there, not academic."

"Bob," said Maggie sweetly, "would you like a cookie with that?"

He selected one and placed it carefully on his saucer.

Then Gretchin said, "Any developments on the Osipov thing?"

After taking a sip of his tea, "Yes, actually, there has been news. I am happy to report that the Agency has agreed to, uh, have him back."

"What made them change their mind?"

"I'm not sure, Gretchin. But anyway, I e-mailed, uh, Mr. Osipov, with an offer, and I'm sorry to say that he turned it down."

"Yeah," she shot back, "I believe you, Bob. You even look sorry. Sure."

He raised his hand. "Now, hear me out, Gretchin. He said that he didn't feel he could do the job properly with, as he put it, and these are his words—with a broken heart. I'm sorry, Gretchin."

She got up and poured herself a cup of tea.

Following her with his eyes, "Does that make you unhappy, Gretchin?"

"It does, Bob."

"Feel free to contact him yourself, but I believe he was simply being honest with himself and candid with me. There would have been a process anyway, paperwork and everything."

She sat down again and sipped the tea. "But not much, right? There was never much paperwork for any of us. Less to shred when we're dead, I guess."

He smiled. "That's a little cynical, Gretchin, and not necessary, I think."

"No, just realistic."

"Well, I'm sorry it didn't work out. Osipov's certainly a great guy."

"And how about someone to help with house-keeping? How about that, Bob?"

He swallowed. "That's a positive, I'm pleased to say. The Agency agreed as to the need, and some-one should be contacting Maggie soon to start with that. They authorized it for once a week."

But she only replied with a dubious *huh* and continued to sip the tea.

That evening, after Bradley and Gretchin had gone out to a movie, Maggie and Packard had gone to the pool for a swim, and Coldgrave had gone to her room to drink and read, Bobbie Lee turned her magazine around for Connors to see and said, "How 'bout a camper?"

The other took it and spread it out on the table. "Seems loike a good idea. But et looks slow. Shouldn't we gat somethin' quicker so's we can use et on the projacts?"

Pulling a chair out and sitting down, "Yeah, we might could do that, but the beauty of usin' a Harley on projects is that it's kind of like a rocket and a jeep put together. I wouldn't want to give that up. Listen, I could git a used camper, like this VW or something, really cheap. It could be an experiment, that's all, and no big loss if it didn't work out." She pulled the magazine back. "Look at that, the top pops up, how rich is that?"

"I've seen them."

"Well, you don't seem too enthusiastic, girl. It was your complaint that got me to lookin' for somethin' with a heater."

"Me lag's gattin' batter. Maybe I could gat used to the boike again."

"Ah, come on, you never did like ridin' in the winter. With a camper bus, winter's nothin'. And long distance is whipped, too. If we pooled our money, we could git one real cheap. I'm a good trader. What say?"

"I'll t'ink about et."

"Well, you do that, 'cause I'm damn sure tired of you gittin' yoursilf shot all the time and tryin' to convalesce on a Harley. I don't like complainers, but I'd be complainin', too. Convalescin' in a camper'd be nothin'. Hell, you could go ahead and git yoursilf shot on jist about every projict."

"Foine. Pick one out."

Bobbie Lee took the magazine and closed it. "That's jist it," she said, "I want you to come look at it with me. I've already called a couple of dealers, and there's some used ones out there. How 'bout tomorrow?"

"Sher."

"Gotcha, girl. We're leavin' at ten. See you at breakfast at eight."

In June the heat moved in in force, with the pool again becoming the general gathering place for launching the day's activities. But if the day began there, it often ended there with an evening swim.

Toward the end of the month, Packard, who had begun to complain that so much swimming was making him feel waterlogged, suggested to Maggie that they take a week and go to the mountains. Her alternative suggestion was to go for a week to Italy. He acquiesced, and she bought him a bottle of whiskey and began to pack.

While they were gone, Gretchin and Bradley left to take a second honeymoon, this time in Aruba. Although unhappy that the idea of taking a second honeymoon had been hers, he decided to be positive about it by joking that since they had tried everything as newlyweds, they were now going to try getting skin cancer together.

Around the same time, Coldgrave left to spend a week in New York with family and friends. While putting her luggage into the Bentley, she declared that although she was a city girl, she might follow up her visit with a few days in the rustic Adirondacks. But if even that failed to cheer her up, she would just go to Marseilles, as there was no place on earth like the Riviera to make one happy.

As these events left Bobbie Lee and Connors to care for things at the Estate, their planned first trip in the newly acquired camper was postponed. Daily, however, Bobbie Lee continued to search the internet for possible campgrounds where the two could vacation.

"I've got it," she announced on a hot day in early July, while lounging poolside with her tablet. "We're goin' to Maine, how 'bout that? Look at these here pictures, girl. Ever been to Acadia?"

Connors sat up and pulled a beer from the ice bucket. Taking the tablet, she said, "Et's too broight out here, I can't see a fuckin' t'ing. I'll joost take your word for et. Sounds good, start packin'."

"Hot damn! Yes!" was the reply. "And reach me one of them beers."

CHAPTER 27

Acadia National Park, July 2016

"Lordy," breathed Bobbie Lee, giving the steering wheel a light punch. "This is one buster of a line, ain't it? We've been here an hour. I'd better git to see a bear tear apart a tourist or two, after all this trouble."

Yawning, Connors reached for her bottle of spring water. She sat up and looked out the windshield. "Are we there yat?"

"No, that's what I'm sayin', look at the line. And we've been here since eight. And here's the ranger, look at this. Sit up straight, wouldya? Come on now, pay attintion, girl."

"Hello, ma'am," said the woman, "just letting everyone know, we're cutting the line off after the car behind yours, so you're okay. It'll be about another half hour or so, but you'll get in. Campsite choice will be bad, but you'll get one, okay?"

"Sure," replied Bobbie Lee, putting her window up as the woman moved to the car behind. "Think of that," she said, "all this waitin' and now we git a shitty campsite. Shit!"

"Don't be profane."

"You're tellin' me not to be profane? Why do you always do that? Git real, girl."

Within an hour they were parked on a site and Bobbie Lee was cranking up the canvas top. Connors had gone to the restroom and was now returning, her bottle of water tipped up.

"That's et," she said, sticking her head into the open door, "I'm out of water. Guess I'll have to gat beer."

"Ain't allowed."

"Lat's find a pub."

Letting the pop button click home, "Ain't one close, prob'ly. You'll jist have to rough it."

When evening moved in, Bobbie Lee took one of the bundles of wood they had bought from a roadside vendor and built a fire in the ring. Using sticks, they roasted marshmallows and ate them as the stars began to peep through the trees. From surrounding campsites came the sounds of conversations and laughter as people became vociferous, and of guitar playing and singing as people loosened up. As the deep Acadian darkness began to settle in upon the campground, the air became charged with a kind of magic.

"Can you feel it, girl?" queried Bobbie Lee as she licked at a marshmallow she had just drawn from the fire. "That's the real deal. You only git that with campin'."

"Feel what?"

"Jeez, girl. The enchantment of the forest."

The reply was apathetic grunt.

"You mean you can't feel it—the stuff, the love of nature, the beauty of it all?"

"Not sher I can."

Spitting on the ground, "Well, it's so thick you could cut it with a knife."

"I believe you."

"That's good, because I despise people who don't love campin'."

When it was late and they had gone to bed, Bobbie Lee looked out through her screened window and said, "This is so pritty out here. It's all been worth it, right?"

"What's been worth what?"

"Come on, you're not gittin' it. I mean, the joy has been worth the trouble and shit of doin' the trip. Waitin' in that long line."

"Well, sher. But I'd sell me soul for some alcohol."

"We'll git some tomorrow, don't worry. We'll drive into Bar Harbor, that's the big deal place. But isn't this pritty right here?"

"Aye, et is."

"And the air's real clear, right? I mean, except for the shit from campfires. And even that's kind of nice."

"Et's clear, you're roight."

"And you'd rather be doin' this than sleepin' in a tint beside a motorcycle, right?"

"You're roight on the nail, there."

Momentarily, "Killy?"

"What?"

"What do you want most in life?"

"Not sher. Maybe to shoot better."

Shaking her head to herself, she said, "But what else? How 'bout the deep, important things, what you're afraid of, what you want?"

"I joost want to go home to me ma."

"Well, there you go, all right, I can see that. What else? Want marriage and a family, anything like that?"

Hesitating, "Et's never seemed to be an option."

"But if it was? That's what I'm askin'."

Connors gave her nose a scratch. "Maybe. . . . But I joost can't imagine lettin' some obnoxious bastard climb all over me."

"Yeah, me neither. Anything else?"

A sigh. "Maybe joost to die en peace."

"Peace?"

"Not loike Martina."

"I sympathize with you there, girl. But I prob'ly won't die the way I want to. It jist doesn't work that way. Nature doesn't love us, does it?"

Connors gave her nose another scratch. "No, et doesn't love us. We only love each other."

The Estate

"It's crazy," remarked Bradley, watching Gretchin swim laps with Maggie, "how women swim. Did you ever notice?"

"No," came the surly reply, "never did. Looks to me, they're just pushing water behind them, like everybody else does, bub."

"No, but look at them—they're elegant."

Packard, without replying, uncapped the bottle, then poured a fresh inch in his glass. Recapping the bottle, he set it aside, picked up the glass, sloshed the whiskey over the ice, and took a thoughtful drink. He too now watched the women swimming. A swim was just a swim, what else could it be? After a moment, he looked away to where the dogs were gnawing on bones. All his life he had avoided deep thinking, as he was much too practical a guy to waste time on such activity. Now here was Bradley, of all people, a practical guy if ever there was one, asking him to consider how their wives were swimming. Jesus!

"You're missing it," said Bradley, running a hand over his crew cut.

Packard grimaced. "What the hell am I missing, tell me? And make it short, I've got drinkin' to do here, pal."

"I already told you, Len. You're missing the elegance of women swimming."

"Hey, you're pullin' my dick, bub. I don't know what you mean by elegance anyway. So, whatever you're talking about, explain it, point to it, show me, or don't ask me again."

Bradley looked at him. "You're too practical. And you know what? You're pragmatic."

"Same thing, pal. Take my advice, stop thinking, and just watch 'em swim."

"Gretchin says she wants me to do more thinking. I've been trying to look more at the artistic side of things."

Belching, "You'll never measure up, bub, trust me."

"Yeah, maybe not with Gretchin."

"Yeah, maybe not."

The women continued to swim, then stopped and reached for the side to catch their breath.

"Come on in," said Maggie, treading water, "it's really nice. You can't just sit and drink. That's not life, that's existence."

"Yeah," chimed Gretchin, "there are only so many cars and guns to talk about."

"Nah," replied Bradley, reaching for his beer, "we're doing all right. We'll just watch you guys. You're elegant."

But she merely gave him an odd look and swam away.

Marseilles, France

Coldgrave reached for her purse, looked at her phone, then swiped it and said, "Yes, Bob. . . . I'm fine, thank you. How are you? . . . I'm in Marseilles, Bob, with friends, drinking. . . . Yes, France. . . . Yes, it's beautiful. . . . It is blue, yes. . . . Uh-huh. . . . Oh, has it been that long? My, I lose track of time, don't I? . . . I'm having fun, that's all I can say. So, what can I do for you, Bob? . . . But why did you use this line, it's my smartphone? . . . I have no idea. When they work, they work, otherwise they don't. I can try calling you back, if you like. . . . Okay, just a minute." Here she left her friends and took a seat at another table. "Yes, go ahead, Bob, I'm listening. . . . Yes, it's secure. . . . Well, I suppose I could be home in, say, twenty-four hours or so. But I'm not one to rush, you know—finish my drink and all. . . . All right, I'll give it a try. If I have a problem, I'll give you a call. . . . Yes, I will, but if it doesn't work, should I just use this phone? . . . All right. . . . Yes, see you then."

Unhurriedly she then returned to her friends. took up her glass, and asked them to continue with their story.

New York City

As she opened the door and stepped inside, she looked up on force of habit, but of course, it wasn't there, for she had hung it on her wall at the Estate.

"Miss your old office, huh?" came a voice.

"No, Bob," she said, turning around, "I don't."

"Then why even open the door?"

"I'm not sure."

"Maybe you're just being nostalgic."

"Possibly."

"It's funny that they haven't reassigned it. Maybe they're expecting to have you back soon." And when she said nothing, "The meeting's been cancelled. Sorry, it looks like you came home for nothing."

A faint smile.

"Anyway," he continued, pulling at his tie, "would you like to go out for a drink?"

"I'm very tired. I think I might just head along home."

"To your parents?"

"No, I meant to the team. But I am tired, thanks."

He looked at her. She did look weary, but not disheveled, never that. It must be a fact of life that beautiful women travel well. "Yeah," he said, "the seats in planes don't let you relax."

"Mine seemed spacious."

"Oh, right, you probably always fly first class. Yeah, that's nice. . . . Come on, just a drink. I'll tell you what the meeting was going to be about."

She looked at the tie, the suit, the manicured trim around the ears. "All right, Bob, why not? Where shall we go?"

Twenty minutes later, as they sat across from each other at a table he said, "You like this place."

"How do you know? Oh, I'm sorry, that's right, they watch us in the shower, as Gretchin would say."

"Yes," he responded. "I mean, no. I mean, I know because it's in your file."

"And files can't be misleading?"

A chuckle. "Sure. But actually, the secretary at the front desk reported that you used to frequent this bar." As she said nothing to this, he looked at her shooting gloves, then said, "Sorry, but yeah, we spy on each other, don't we?"

"Sounds like a confession."

He reached for his Coke and took a drink, his eyes upon her hair, her face. She took up her glass of Nolet's, put it to her nose for a moment, then took a sip.

"I have a question," he said. "How would you like to go to a Labor Day picnic?"

"That sounds rustic."

"Not really. My church is having it. I was wondering if you would like to go . . . with me."

"Labor Day," she said. "That's the military one?"

"No, that would be Memorial Day, Mary. That's earlier, we already had that."

"In July?"

"No, that's Independence Day. Labor Day is at the beginning of September, to get people in the mood for autumn."

"Yes, like Halloween. I've done that. That's with the masks."

His eyes went closed. Then he said, "This would be a picnic, during the day. Hot dogs, hamburgers, stuff like that. It's fun. I think you would like it."

"Yes, rustic. I've done that. Those things are fun."

Brightening, "Well, so, would you like to go?"

She looked at him. "I think I will pass on this party, Bob. But it was nice of you to ask me."

Momentarily, "We're the same age, you know."

"Yes."

"We have a lot in common, I was thinking. Have you ever thought that?" He watched as she shook her head, raised the glass to her lips, took a drink, then set it in front of her, as if to mark something between them. "Well, we do," he continued. "We're the same age, we're in the same profession, we—"

"Go to the same posh bar?"

Momentarily, "Could I ask you something else? This may sound strange, but have you ever had any feelings for me?"

"No."

He looked down at her glass, then back up at her, and said, "All right."

"And thank you for asking me to the party, Bob, but I do not wish to go."

"Picnic," he corrected.

"Whatever."

He nodded. "Sure, okay. Thanks for being straight up with me about it."

Finishing her drink, she said, "There was no meeting, was there?"

He looked down and answered, "No." Then, looking up at her, "I guess you did come home early for nothing."

"Yes."

"So," he said, "would you like another drink?"

"No. But thank you for asking, Bob."

"So, you're going home now?"

"Yes. Maggie said she'll have the tea on."

He blinked. "The tea. Right."

"After a drive, there's nothing like a good cup of tea."

www.ingramcontent.com/pod-product-compliance
Lightning Source LLC
Chambersburg PA
CBHW071603110726
47908CB00007B/2227